TALES *from a*
TALKING BOARD

TALES *from a*
TALKING BOARD

EDITED BY
ROSS E. LOCKHART

WORD HORDE
PETALUMA, CA

Tales from a Talking Board
© 2017 by Ross E. Lockhart
This edition of *Tales from a Talking Board*
© 2017 by Word Horde

Cover art and design © 2017 by Yves Tourigny

Edited by Ross E. Lockhart

An extension of this copyright page appears on page 209

First Edition

ISBN: 978-1-939905-35-2

A Word Horde Book
www.wordhorde.com

TABLE OF CONTENTS

Tales from a Talking Board is dedicated to…

Elijah Bond
William Fuld
Emily Grant Hutchings
Pearl Curran
Jane Roberts

…all of whom were consulted in the creation of this volume.

"Let no one be found among you who sacrifices his son or daughter in the fire, who practices divination or sorcery, interprets omens, engages in witchcraft, or casts spells, or who is a medium or spiritist or who consults the dead. Anyone who does these things is detestable to the Lord."

—Deut. 18:10–12, NIV

"Ages 8 to Adult."

—Ouija board packaging, 1972

A BRIEF HISTORY OF TALKING BOARDS

ROSS E. LOCKHART

Not long before the Civil War, a movement swept across the United States, one that held the belief that not only did the soul continue to exist after the death of the body, but that these souls, these *spirits*, could be communicated with, and could impart wisdom, warnings, and pathways to better connect the living with a supernatural, infinite intelligence. This movement, known as Spiritualism, flourished, boasting nearly eight million followers worldwide by the turn of the twentieth century, despite holding no central doctrine, no canonical texts, and no formal organization.

Initially appearing in upstate New York, birthplace of religious movements such as Millerism, Adventism, and Mormonism, Spiritualism boasted its celebrities—the Fox Sisters, Cora L. V. Scott, Achsa W. Sprague, and Paschal Beverly Randolph, to name a few—but a big part of its appeal was its promise to put the power of spirit communication into the hands of its adherents. Advancing technology and American entrepreneurial spirit intervened, and complex divinatory systems like spirit cabinets, table turnings, and alphabetical knockings soon gave way to simpler, more foolproof methods.

First came the *planchette* in 1853, a "little plank" of heart-shaped wood with a pencil incorporated, a means of channeling spirits through automatic writing. Time passed, and Spiritualists and entrepreneurs continued to refine the technology of Spiritualism. In 1886, the Associated Press reported on a new phenomenon sweeping through Spiritualist circles, the "talking board," a tray with the letters of the alphabet imprinted upon it, on which a planchette (sans pencil) would be used to point to individual letters at the urging of the spirits.

Inspired by this development, Charles Kennard of Baltimore brought together a group of investors, including attorney Elijah Bond and painter/varnisher William Fuld, to form the Kennard Novelty Company to produce and market these talking boards.

While Fuld was the artist, Kennard and Bond are better described as capitalists than Spiritualists. They saw an opportunity to make money, so in traditional American spirit, they jumped at it. But that didn't stop them from asking their board to name itself. Working with Bond's sister-in-law Helen Peters as medium, they asked the board its name. The board spelled out O-U-I-J-A. The investors puzzled over this strange word. What could it mean? They put the question to Peters. The board answered: "Good luck."

Or so the legend goes. Whether the Ouija board named itself, or if the name comes from the French and German words for yes (oui, ja), or if Peters subconsciously (or consciously) named the board in honor of the popular women's rights activist Ouida remains enshrouded in mystery, but in 1891, Bond was awarded U. S. Patent number 446,054 and the Kennard Novelty Company Ouija board officially went into production.

In 1892, William Fuld patented his own improved version of the talking board (Patent no. 479,266). Fuld's mystifying oracle incorporated magnetized wires as a way of providing an early force-feedback effect, and promised to "form words which constitute questions that the players must answer before the board will reply to the previous question." Fuld would spend the next several years patenting and copyrighting several improvements to his board, securing his reputation as the Father of the Ouija board.

Countless variations on the talking board have been produced in the more than 130 years since its inception, bearing names like J.E. Garside's *Throne Board* (1893), Southern Toy Company's *Quija* (1919), J. W. Stanley's *Witchy Board* (1920), Fortune Industries' *Wizard* (1940s), Cardinal's *Swami* (1940s), Clinton Art Products' *Rajah* (1944), and Pacific Game Company's *Predicta* (1968).

For much of their history, talking boards were treated as a harmless parlor game, celebrated in song and depicted by Norman Rockwell on the cover of the *Saturday Evening Post*. But as time passed, more sinister Ouija stories appeared. Sensationalist newspaper accounts linked Ouija boards to crimes, even murders, and mental illness. In 1971, author William Peter Blatty included scenes featuring a Ouija board in his novel *The Exorcist*, and that scene's inclusion in William Friedkin's 1973 film adaptation, as young Regan MacNeil uses the board to chat with Captain Howdy/Pazuzu, may have been the catalyst that pushed the talking board from innocent game to Satanic tool in the minds of the American public. Regardless, talking boards remain popular, though marketing has shifted considerably towards darker themes, with Ouija-branded horror films, and an emphasis on the idea that *it's just a game...or is it?*

My first encounter with Ouija would have been in the late 1970s in a parochial school in southern California. Let me clarify, this was not my first encounter with a Ouija board in the flesh (that would be a few years later), but an encounter with what I call the Ouija board story.

During a bit of classroom free time, a group of kids started talking about Ouija boards, perhaps echoing a parent's echoing of a Sunday sermon, or an adult conversation over how *The Exorcist* had scared the Hell out of them. The conversation became heated, prompting the teacher to intervene. Now, this teacher could have dispelled the rumors of spirits and demons being bandied about

the classroom. She could have calmed our fears, quelled our con-
cerns, but instead, she decided to grab the planchette and run with
it, spinning a horrifying tale of the time a Ouija board showed
up in the school's kindergarten toy box, and how this board was
somehow manipulated by the motley collection of five-year-olds
into summoning a phantasmagoric fantasia of nightmare appari-
tions, spinning about the room like a magic lantern carousel. As I
recall, the story climaxed in blood and tears, as the spirits reached
their claws through the veil to rend and disassemble a particularly
wicked little boy (and I'd swear the teacher looked directly at me
at this point), spattering the other children with gore and gristle
before the previously absent teachers (seriously, where were they
this whole time?) could intervene. But intervene they did, grabbing the board (and, presumably, the planchette) and carrying it
out into the playground where it was promptly burned, sanitized
in cleansing, sacred fire.

When the teacher finished her account, I looked around the
classroom, taking in the shellshocked faces of my suddenly silent
classmates. I thought long about the story, adding the pieces together, then looked at my teacher, her arms crossed in front of
her chest. It didn't add up. There was no barren, scorched spot on
the playground in front of the kindergarten classroom. And most
kindergarteners didn't really have the motor or language skills to
manipulate and properly utilize a Ouija board. In that moment,
I realized the teacher was putting us on, telling a tall tale, lying
to a group of kids in order to scare us. But to what ends? To keep
us on the straight and narrow? To scare us away from the occult?
To make us compliant, unquestioning Christians? As my peers sat
agape, aghast, I realized the absurdity of it all. I started laughing,
uncontrollably…

…and spent the rest of the day in the principal's office.

And with that brief account of Ouija and personal history, I
welcome you, reader, to *Tales from a Talking Board*, an anthology
exploring the history, the present, and the future of talking boards

and other, stranger tools of divination and spirit communication. Herein, you will find fourteen weird and wonder-filled tales of the strange and supernatural, by fourteen of my favorite authors. So dim the light, place the board across your knees, and ever so gingerly, press your fingers against the planchette. Now relax, and think of a question. The spirits have a lot to tell you...

Ross E. Lockhart
Petaluma, CA
July, 2017

"YESNOGOODBYE"

KRISTI DEMEESTER

Cassandra found the Ouija board in her dad's attic. Her mom had left a year ago, right after her thirteenth birthday, and her dad had packed everything up that might have her mother's stain still on it.

"I'm not supposed to go up there," she said and shook her head so her dark braids fell over her face. I wanted to reach out and touch her cheeks and her mouth every time she did that, but I kept my hands pinned against my thighs and reminded myself that she would probably think it was weird.

"Bet it's not even real," I said, but even as I spoke, I knew it was. The board was a dark, heavy wood and smelled of ancient dust and quiet places where things are put to be forgotten. Kind of like Cassandra's mom. She wouldn't talk about her, and I never asked because she was my best friend, and you don't say things to make your best friend sad.

The letters were etched deep in the wood and were the color of something burnt. In the upper corners were two smiling skulls. Their teeth were sharp and pointed, and I forced myself to look at them even though there was something like fear coming awake and crawling in my belly.

"Jesus, Dee. I mean look at this thing. It's creepy as fuck. It's the real deal," she said, and I marveled at how easily the curse word rolled off her tongue. Like it was nothing. Like she didn't even think of it, and I watched her mouth, and then she saw me looking, and I pretended to be looking at the board.

"I guess so."

"Whatever. You're going to do it with me, right?"

"Yeah. Hell yeah," I said, testing the word in my mouth, but it felt sour and awkward, and Cassandra twisted away from me to hide her smirk, and I wished I could have melted into the floor.

"Okay. We have to do this right, though. Be right back," she said and dashed out of the room. My hands were damp, and I swiped them against my jeans and then smoothed my hair and tried to ignore the rabbit-quick beat of my heart inside my chest.

When Cassandra came back in, she carried a few candles and tucked under her arm was a glass bottle filled with a deep purple liquid. "To set the mood," she said and placed the candles around the Ouija board and then lifted the bottle to her lips and swallowed. I watched her throat and all of my secret places went damp.

"Here." She pushed the bottle at me, and I lifted it and took a sniff.

"This is wine, isn't it?"

She rolled her eyes. "Don't be such a wuss. Just drink some."

I tipped the bottle back and tried not to cough, and she nodded and grinned, and so I drank some more, and she grabbed me by the shoulders, and her breath smelled sweet, and I leaned into her and laughed.

"So, what do we ask it?" She lit the candles one by one with a lighter she'd pulled from her pocket and sank back on her heels.

I knew what it was I wanted to ask it, but I wouldn't. "I don't know. Something stupid. Just to see if it even works."

Cassandra held her hands out and grasped the small triangle on the board between us. There was a hole through the middle so you could see the letters, and she placed her fingers on the edges.

"Well, come on," she said, and I did the same, and my fingers were just barely touching hers. She giggled and cleared her throat. "Is anyone there?"

We watched the little triangle, but it didn't move. "Hello?" she said and still nothing happened, and I opened my mouth to tell her it wasn't working, to tell her this was stupid and couldn't we just watch old movies the way we always did, and then our fingers were moving and the little hole went up and up until we looked through and saw.

Yes.

"You did that," I said, but Cassandra shook her head, and she smelled like cinnamon, and it made my entire body hurt.

"Did you?" she said.

"No." A grin split her lips, and she waggled her eyebrows.

"Told you it would work."

"So ask it something else."

"What's my name?" she said, and we watched as the triangle traced over the C, the A, and S, and Cassandra laughed, high and clear.

"You're pushing it. Of course you know how to spell your own name."

"Then you ask it something. Something no one knows but you. A secret. That way, we'll know it's for real," she said, and my neck went all warm, and I could feel the red creeping into my face. Because I had a secret. A secret that felt too heavy for my mouth. But I wouldn't ask that question.

I tried to think of something Cassandra didn't already know about me, but there wasn't much. I never felt like I knew as much about her as she did about me. She'd listen to me go on and on and then get real quiet, and I didn't want to make her mad, so I never asked that many questions.

Every Friday she'd ask me to come over and then on Saturdays she came home with me, and my mom didn't care. Thought it was nice that I had a good friend, and her dad was never home to ask questions. Cassandra never really talked about him either.

Sometimes, I wondered if he even existed. If she just lived in that big house all alone and pretended. But sometimes she'd have bruises on her arms or on her neck, and she'd stop talking for a few days, and I would let her be quiet. I never minded.

"Got it. And don't move your hands," she said. I looked away from the board. I didn't want to see my fingers moving or Cassandra's face when I asked my question.

"What do I keep under my pillow? While I sleep?"

Our fingers moved, and I could feel the warmth of her skin, and Cassandra spelled out the letters one by one, and by the fourth letter, I knew the board was real and jerked backward.

"It's right, isn't it?" Cassandra squealed, and I didn't want to play that game anymore. "What do you keep under your pillow?"

"It's nothing. A bracelet my grandma gave me before she died," I said, but it was a lie. It was the friendship bracelet Cassandra gave me last summer. I'd never taken it off, not even to take a shower, and when it finally disintegrated, I tucked the pieces into a sandwich bag and stuck it under my pillow.

"My turn. Are you a boy or a girl?" Cassandra said, and I wanted to tell her not to ask it that, that it wasn't smart to know anything about whatever was inside the board, but the triangle moved, and there was nothing I could do.

G-I-R-L.

"You ask it something," Cassandra said, but I stayed quiet, and she rolled her eyes at me. "Fine. How old were you when you died?"

The triangle shifted to the line of numbers at the bottom of the board and hovered over the one and then the six.

"Sixteen," Cassandra said, and the triangle moved to show us *Yes*. "Did you live here? In this house?" The triangle showed us *No*.

Cassandra fluttered her fingers against mine and smiled. "What's your name?"

"Don't ask what its name is!" My voice was hoarse, and I coughed.

"Why not?" Cassandra said. I wasn't sure why I'd said that, but the triangle was finding the letters anyway.

M-A-R-I-A-N-N-E

"How did you die?" Cassandra said, and it was like all the air had been sucked out of the room, and I couldn't breathe, and I wanted to run out of there and out of the house until my lungs went raw, but I sat and watched the triangle.

H-U-R-T-D-Y-O-

Cassandra frowned. "That doesn't make any sense," she said, and the triangle moved again.

H-U-R-T-D-A-D-S-A-M-E-A-S-M-E

Cassandra lifted her hands off of the triangle and cracked her knuckles one by one. "Ask it something else," I said. She put her hands back down.

"Okay, great spirits of the unknown beyond. Is someone in love with me?" The triangle slid up and to the left. *Yes.*

She laughed, and another part of me unraveled. There was a window behind Cassandra, and I focused on that. Looked out into the dark so I wouldn't have to look at her.

"Who's in love with me?" she said, and my guts turned to water. The triangle jerked under my hands, and I looked away.

No.

"No? What's that supposed to mean?" she said. Underneath the little hole, the word looked large and accusatory. Cassandra took her hands off the triangle so she could tuck her braids behind her ear.

Under my fingers, the triangle jumped, and I started and pulled away. The triangle continued to move, and we both stared down at it.

D-O-N-T, the triangle spelled and then stopped for a second before it started up again.

D-O-N-T-D-A-D-D-Y-H-U-R-T. Again and again, the triangle spelled out the phrase. *Don'tDaddyHurt. Don'tDaddyHurt.*

Cassandra made a sound like the one our dog, Buster, made when he cut his leg on some barbed wire. She kicked the board so

the triangle went flying and the board landed upside down next to
her bed. Her face was wet, and she turned away.

"What was—"

"Nothing," she said, and her voice was hard edges, and I forced
my tongue to be still.

She blew out the candles and grabbed the bottle of wine, tipped
it back, and drank until she spluttered. Her mouth was the color
of blood.

"Come on. Let's go watch a movie or something," she said and
left the room, and I watched the place where her body used to be.
The window was still dark, and I thought I saw something move
against it. A hand flexed against the glass or a mouth opening,
but there was nothing there, and I stood and left the board and
triangle on the floor and hurried out of the room.

We watched movies for the rest of the night. Every few minutes,
Cassandra would take a pull off of the bottle and pretty soon she
was giggling and poking at me, and I would slap her hand away
even if what I really wanted to do was wrap my fingers around hers
and never let go. Eventually, we fell asleep on the couch.

When I woke up, the house was dark, and the television was
turned off. I rolled over and looked for Cassandra, but she wasn't
there. I held my breath.

The sound was soft at first. Like the very start of someone sigh-
ing before it catches in their throat. "Cass?" I called into all of that
gathered dark, but nothing answered me, and I swung my legs
over the couch.

It's nothing, I told myself and forced myself to stand—my hands
groping before me—and moved toward the hallway. "Cass?" I said
again, and I could hear her then, her voice low and growling, as
she mumbled, and I followed the sound to her bedroom. She faced
away from me. She'd taken off her all of her clothes. Bare-backed
with her thighs and calves clenched as she stood on tiptoe and
pressed her lips to the window. Whispered to whatever lay behind
the glass.

"It isn't a ghost. What we let out of the board. It's something else. How many times do you think it tried to get in? Before we opened the door?" she said, and I could smell her then. Like urine and sweat, and I brought my hand over my mouth. "I think it was like him. Like Daddy. It was always going to find a way. Didn't matter if you locked the door or not. It never fucking mattered."

"What are you talking about?" I said, and she turned to me then, her eyes glittering, and stepped forward.

"Come and see."

"There's nothing out there. It's just a window."

"Only if you don't know where to look." She held out her hand, and I couldn't help it. There was still the need to touch her lying underneath all of my hot, damp fear, and I let her wrap her fingers over mine and pull me beside her.

"See?" she said and pressed her face and her mouth against the glass.

I closed my eyes. Cassandra pushed her hip against mine, and I remembered her skin was bare, and my entire body shuddered. "He doesn't come home when you're here. With me."

Behind me, something clattered. The sound of wood grating against wood, and I wondered if the board had somehow righted itself. If it was spelling out dead secrets. I opened my eyes and squinted into the dark at the shape taking form there.

"I taught myself how to disappear. How to make it so it's like I'm not even there. So I won't lose myself inside of him. He always calls me his girl when he's done, but I'm not. I'm not his girl," she said, and together we watched the darkness shift into something that looked like teeth. "I've thought about how to kill him. Over and over until it's almost like I've already done it. But they'd send me away because I'd mess it up, and they would know I'd done it. They'd send me away from you. And if you weren't there anymore, I think I'd forget how to breathe."

I wondered if she could hear my heart. If she knew all the beautiful words I'd left to die on my tongue. Because she carried them inside of her, too. Delicate, breakable things hidden in our tightly clutched fists.

"Do you see it? There?" She lifted a finger and traced it over the glass, and I looked. I saw. Mouth and teeth and tongue all locked together. A great maw opened wide, and I wondered if we screamed, if it would swallow the sound down and then give it back to us as something better. Something lovely.

"We let it out of the board. We won't ever be able to put it back. I don't think I want to," she said and turned so that her breath fell warm over my cheeks and then pressed her lips to my neck. "Don't tell anyone. About him. About what he does. They'll take me away," she said, and my cheeks were wet with her tears, and I nodded my head.

"I won't," I said, and the words were like ground glass in my mouth.

Again, the board rattled behind us, and we went to it, watched as the triangle passed over the letters.

Don'tDaddyHurt.

Cassandra's breath came hard, and she bent down and placed her fingers against the triangle and spoke to the board. "Could you do it? If I asked you to? Could you make it look like an accident, and then maybe my mom would come back, and I wouldn't have to leave?" She licked her lips and fidgeted, and I knew what it was she was asking. I didn't stop her. I wanted him dead, too.

Her desperation hung over her like something heavy, and she looked up at me, and I'd never wanted something so bad in my entire life. I wanted it for her. Wanted it to pull him inside out and leave him a smeared pile of stinking guts.

I couldn't see the triangle, but I heard it moving over the board. When it stopped, I heard Cassandra's breath as it whooshed out of her. She slumped forward.

"It can't help us. Can it?" I asked. Fingers appeared against the glass, a swirl of hair, and then there was the sound of someone crying or laughing. I couldn't tell which.

"No." She picked the board up and threw it against the far wall where it clattered to the floor. "Goddammit. Godammit!" Before I could move, she was at the window again, her fist drawn back, and then she brought it shuddering down, and I heard the sound of bone cracking, and there was blood on her fingers.

"Why won't you help me? Why come out of the board if you can't help?" she screamed and there was nothing to answer her.

My face was wet when I crawled to her and pulled her down so that her head rested on my shoulder. Whatever it was inside of the board, I hated it. Hated it for hurting her, hated it for the things it wouldn't give her. Hated myself because I couldn't give them to her either.

She traced her mouth along my jaw and then pressed her lips against mine. She tasted of cherries and wine, and everything inside of me came roaring awake. The entire world lit up in shades of crimson and violet.

I kissed her back. Curved my body to hers and cupped her chin with my hands and then locked what she'd told me about her father away. Pushed it into the parts of myself that would one day become a ghost. I fell into her and opened my mouth to all of the darkness gathering outside of her window.

"It's like drowning," she said and breathed into me, and I filled myself full of her and prayed to whatever was outside of the window. Asked that if it could do nothing else, that it would help me keep her there, hidden away inside of me.

"When we're older, I'll take you away," I said, and I could feel her smile. She wrapped her fingers in my hair.

"Yes," she said.

THE DEVIL AND THE BUGLE BOYS

J. M. MCDERMOTT

By day, we marched and practiced for the competitions every few days; at night, we slept on a filthy bus until we reached a high school gymnasium, where we scattered into sleeping bags until daylight came. It was three months of marching and music, an escape and an adventure for all of us high school kids. I had been hardcore in music all my life, hopping from instrument to instrument until I fell in love with the huge steel beast that moaned like how I imagined dinosaurs would sound if they could sing: the tuba, which was the contrabass bugle for the corps. My last year at it, I felt myself falling through the edges of performances, had bad dreams on the bus, and I couldn't sleep much on the hard gymnasium floors anymore. A couple of the drummers had trouble sleeping, too, but it looked like too much Red Bull and uppers and an excuse to smoke pot out in the bushes. A couple of the horn players were like me, in their way. Isaac, one of my contrabass bugle buddies, slept really well on the buses, for some reason. He tumbled out to the gymnasium floors refreshed and bored, reading a little, maybe. Staring off into the rafters and listening to the rustling of whoever was sneaking out to smoke pot or have sex before official bedtime ended. Lance was a strict Mormon, and he had trouble sleeping, period. It was hard on him. He was young, about fifteen. He was way out of his comfort zone. I was the contrabass bugle section leader, and I had tried to take Lance under my wing. The road was not friendly to him. I was surprised he didn't wash out the second week. Yet, there he was, tossing and turning on the gymnasium floor. I was in my third year of it—my last year—and I had planned ahead for my restless nights with some books and board games that were heavy, but worth it to me, to keep me feeling rooted in something outside of music. I was never going to be a musician. I was never going to play after this season. About halfway through, I didn't know why I even came back for one more summer in the sun. I saw no future in music, no future playing the tuba. They were expensive, and I was poor. There was no band to join in my little town, no one wanted to hear it sing. I was going to get a job next summer, and just keep working, and push all the dreams away. I was contrabass bugle section leader, and I was awake in the dark, looking around for anyone who might want to sit out at the edge of the gym, where the light from the bathrooms would illuminate a quiet game of something until it was time to eat and get back out into the fields for practice.

I caught the eye of Isaac, and nodded at him. I pointed at my box and the hallway door to the locker rooms, where we could do something besides sleep and stare into darkness. He grabbed Lance on the way out by kicking the kid in the leg. Lance was awake. It wasn't a hard kick, or a cruel one. It was the kind you do to push someone towards a little scrap of joy in the dark.

So, we went out into the hall between the gymnasium and the locker rooms, and opened the box up.

"Nothing loud," said Isaac.

"I got something real quiet. Y'all are both good kids. You ever summon anything?"

"I'm not touching that," said Lance.

"So don't touch it. Someone needs to do the pad and pen."

"Serously, dude?" said Isaac.

"It's cool. I've done this a bunch. I've still got all my fingers and toes. Expect a bunch of lies, with a little truth."

"I don't know, Stephen…"

"Is your faith not stronger than a stupid piece of plastic? Relax. It's not even real."

"How do you know?"

"Isaac, are you brave enough to dance with the devil in the dark?"

He was smiling and shaking his head, but he didn't stop me when I pulled it out of the box and set it up between us. Inside the box was the notepad I kept in there. Isaac and I put our hands on the planchette, and held still, waiting for any passing spirit to find us in that high school hallway somewhere in the Midwest. (I don't even remember where we were by that point in the summer. It's all one big, hot, bug-infested football field from Colorado to Florida, until Finals in Madison, Wisconsin.)

"If you can summon devils with this," said Isaac, "can you summon angels?"

The planchette moved. It stated, very clearly, No.

Give it a few seconds, so we can skip over the part where we each accused the other of moving the planchette, and both of us said we didn't. We can skip over some of the early, stupid questions, too.

You can't summon angels with the devil's telephone. You can summon ghosts in creepy, empty high school hallways with all the lockers open in the middle of summer, at night, between the locker rooms and the gymnasium, but this was no ghost. My friends, Isaac and I were talking straight to the bottom of the abyss. Anyone who's ever been to some rural high school in the Midwest would not be surprised to find hell's not far away, for anyone bothering to look. These huge, rural schools, out in the cornfields and soybeans, out where there's barely a tree standing and the humidity pushes all the sweat inside of you down into the grass. Yeah, this is where the devil's going to talk to band nerds in the dark in plastic and cardboard and painted letters.

So, let's get to the good stuff. Lance's hands were shaking while he was writing down letters and taking notes back to us. Isaac was stone-faced, chilled to the bone by what he was hearing the devil tell us. I was smirking. These things are all a game. I believed in God, I think, but not in the power of devils.

"We're asking pussy questions, Isaac. It's the devil. We get it. He's a bad-ass motherfucker, and we've got him on the line. So try to think of a question that doesn't suck."

"Like what?"

The planchette moved to answer. D-E-T-H

"Everyone dies, so I think your suggestion is stupid. Let me ask you this: Will we ever pull ahead of the Blue Regiment?" That was another drum corps we were riding up close to all season. Judges never let us climb up over the top, no matter how hard we practiced and played. There was about a month to go until finals, though, and we were always close.

After a pause, the planchette moved. M-A-B

"I always assumed the devil could spell," I said.

"Don't taunt him," said Isaac. "He said maybe. We're not making any deals with you, so don't even try. It isn't worth it."

H-A-H-A-H-A

"How about telling us which member of the color guard is most likely to deflower our young friend, Lance?"

N-O-N

"Not looking good for you, Lance."

"This is kind of freaking me out, okay?" said Isaac. "Can we stop?"

"Can we? Should we?"

No

"You're moving it, Stephen."

"Am I moving the thing?"

The planchette swirled around and returned. No

"I'm not moving the thing," I said. "Come on, give the devil his due. He can speak for himself. Can't you, bad boy?"

Yes

"All right, let's see if we can make a deal, infernal spirit. I want Lance to get laid this summer. What will it take to seduce a lovely woman for him?"

Let's be totally fair, for a moment, because I didn't really believe in this spiritual shit very much, honestly, and I was looking for some cheap entertainment before sunrise. I began to move the planchette.

P-A-N-T-S I-S-A-A-K D-R-N-G R-U-N T-H-R-U

"That's a lot of letters," I said. "Lance, did you catch that?"

"I got it. Uh. You know, I don't actually care about getting laid this summer."

"Sure you do," said Isaac. "What did it say?"

"It said to pants Isaac during the run through."

"When?"

Me, again, with the planchette in hand. T-O-D-A-Y

"Okay. Who do you want to be the one pantsing him? I can't do it. I'm on the other side of the line from those two."

G-R-L

"Which girl?"

T-H G-R-L

"Okay, I think. So, to get laid, Lance needs to convince the girl he wants to sleep with to pants Isaac during the run through, today?"

Yes

So, I let go of control of the planchette, but my hands stayed on.

The drummers were coming back from smoking weed around the side of the building, and that meant it was getting close to time to get ready.

Isaac saw them and nodded at us. It was time to close up shop. One of the drummers saw us with the Ouija board and gave us the devil horn hand signal of approval. The other crossed himself and shook his head. I think he was a Mormon pothead. We were based out of Denver, so we had a large Mormon contingent in our corps. Isaac was technically Mormon, but I'd seen him drink beer and I know he wasn't a virgin. Lance was strict. It's easy to be strict when you're young.

The planchette moved one last time.

I-T S-T-I-L C-O-U-N-T-S

"What the hell does that mean?" said Isaac.

"I think we just made a deal with the devil, Isaac."

He jumped back from the planchette like it was on fire. "No," he said. "No way. We don't make deals. No way."

"It isn't up to you, is it?" said Lance, thoughtfully. He pulled out the pages of the little notepad and crumpled them up. He handed them over to one of the drummers, who had given us the devil horns. I don't remember his name. I just remember his beard, that he refused to chop all summer, even though it looked horrible. "Can you burn this for me?" said Lance. "It's probably satanic."

He was into it.

So, the big lights turned on, and we all scrambled up groggy from bedrolls on the gymnasium floor, still bone tired and sore, to get some food at the cafeteria truck and get our gear together for the day ahead. We always started with stretching, then some visual rehearsals—marching in formation, that sort of thing. Then, we went out into the field and rehearsed the sets from the show. We didn't play our instruments, yet. We carried them, nothing but shorts and gloves and socks and shoes and a hat on, and this late in the season, hardly any sunblock. We were as bronzed as we were going to be, by midsummer. We sang while we marched, with our little notebooks bouncing off our hips, where we kept track of each spot on the field we were supposed to be. By then, they were mostly ornamental. We knew where we were supposed to be. We knew through muscle memory the shifts in pace and musculature to get through our paces. The drummers played sometimes, but the hornline just sang. We didn't want to blow out our lips, and we wanted to focus on just the visuals. Then, it was lunch time, and we lined up at the food truck, took whatever slop we were given, and sat down in the shade in groups and bunches. Isaac usually sat with us. But, he was off by himself, angry-looking, staring at Lance. Lance usually sat with us, too. The contrabass line was so tight, we took shits together when we could find eight thrones in a row. Now, we were cracked up. Lance and Isaac had been thinking all this time, when we should have been getting better for a show.

Lance was hanging with the drumline, today. I had expected him to be hanging with a woman, honestly, as I had really, at heart, the best of intentions: use my wicked powers of suggestion to encourage Lance to try something racy, get out of his shell a little. Getting pantsed at band camp was basically nothing that didn't happen with some regularity, that many teenagers running around in the heat under pressure to perform. Isaac getting pantsed had happened already, and it didn't seem so traumatic.

This afternoon, we would see, in the run through before we stopped to get ready for the show, if there was a show that night. First, we got into our sections and got our lips warmed up, practiced parts of the show. We stood in a half-circle around the horn director, then broke off into sections. Contrabasses went with the euphoniums, and they had more elaborate parts to work on than we did. Isaac and Lance stood next to each other, in the middle of my line. The mood was sour. I could feel it in the water breaks between notes. After this, we'd do go out onto the field for full rehearsal.

The devil's always in the details, though. A storm blew in that night. It announced itself with thunder and a sudden wind. It was one of those hard, fast summer storms on the prairie that wouldn't last long, but it would last long enough to ruin run throughs for the night, maybe even cause the show to get canceled if the thunder and lightning stuck around and the field was ruined with mud.

The show was canceled, and we spent the evening in horn sectionals scattered around the places in the school where we could stay out of the rain. We got on the bus, all amped up and worked up and I got into my bus box, again, and pulled out the Ouija board to sit with Lance in the aisle while Isaac took notes. Lance wanted to talk to the underworld, and Isaac was pretty freaked out, so he didn't want to touch the damn thing. We had spectators for a little bit, but people had headphones on, had books they were passing around, and stories to tell each other and windows to stare out of. Soon enough, everyone was asleep but us, and we were fading, too.

Of course, the devil would be on the roads at night across the Midwest, where the streetlights were years away from being built, and the decimation of the cornfields brought pestilence and despair unto the souls of lost men, drinking and driving in darkness, dying in darkness. Of course, the devil is there where long travelers fall asleep at the wheel, and teenage boys in drum corps buses call to him on a Ouija board placed on the floor between aisles. The road was bumpy and hard, and it didn't seem like it was working, but the planchette moved a little more than just the road and sway allowed.

"I'm not going to sell my soul over meaningless sex," said Lance. "That was never going to happen. I want to know what you can offer me. What's your best offer?"

No

"Why not?"

N-T-H-W-R-K-S

"I don't understand," said Isaac. Not... How... Works?"

Yes

"How does it work, to sell your soul? What do you get from it?"

N-T-H-N-G

Isaac cocked his head. "You asked what he gets out of it, right? Is that what you asked?"

"No, I mean, if I sell my soul to you," said Lance, "or he does, or anyone, what can you give the person? What can you offer them in exchange? Show me the money."

I-S-P-Y-W-I-T-H-M-Y

Isaac just shook his head. "I don't know, man. This is too weird."

"I don't think I'll be making a deal with this evil spirit," said Lance. "The darkness has no power in this world if we don't let them. Jesus Christ has banished them all."

"Yeah, fuck the devil," I said. "Never take the deal."

"I just wanted to know how much power he had, that's all. I never, for a minute, considered it, Isaac. Your pants were safe."

"Well, fuck you for not telling me that sooner," he said. Isaac and I both knew that we were hearing the end result of a spiritual crisis and Lance had been thinking about it.

We hit a rough patch of highway and the planchette swung wild. We couldn't keep it steady enough for words. It seemed to break the spell between us, and when we put our hands back on the planchette, it stayed limp and unmoving. We waited for a few minutes, and nothing happened.

Isaac fell asleep in the seat above us. I was a veteran, and a section leader. I had enough authority to lay down flat in the aisle, where I could sleep stretched out while the bus rumbled.

I didn't think I was asleep, yet, just getting ready to sleep, when someone thumped me on the head. I shouted out, and sat up, and looked around to see who hit me. Lance and Isaac were awake, too. The only other person on the bus awake was the driver way up at the front.

"Who fucking flicked my ear?" whispered Isaac.

Lance had gotten up into a seat to sleep. He did not have aisle privileges. He was rubbing the back of his head. The two soprano players behind him were way out, leaning on each other and drooling. No way they did anything. I looked around, too.

"That was weird," I said. "He'd need three hands to hit us all at once. We're pretty spread out, too."

The Ouija board was out, and the planchette was resting on the letter 'U'.

I put my hands on the board. "Come on, Lance, let's get this over with so we can go back to sleep."

He looked down at the board and at me. He got very pale.

"Isaac?"

"Fuck no, man."

"Just me, then. Well, fuck you for waking us up. You hear that? You don't scare me. You don't belong here, and you need to fucking leave. Now."

The planchette didn't move. It doesn't work with just one person.

"Lance, you got the guts for this?"

He came and leaned over, but did not sit on the ground. He just leaned over. He placed one hand on the planchette. "What do you want?" he said.

Good-bye

Isaac and Lance and I looked around. "I'm going back to sleep," I said.

I was going to try, anyway.

We woke up when the bus stopped in another high school, at another gymnasium where we'd be crashed out on the hard floor until it was time to wake up for rehearsal, get ready for a show, and maybe not get rained out, again.

I was lying awake, staring at the rafters, thinking about the devil, and about the darkness of everything.

Isaac came over to me and asked to borrow the Ouija board. Lance was with him. I handed it over, but I had no desire to join them. I pulled out some cards from my box and started playing solitaire. They didn't seem to notice. They took the Ouija board away out the door and into the hallway between the locker rooms and the gymnasium, where we weren't supposed to hang out, but did anyway. They told me later that day they had taken the Ouija board out to where the drummers were smoking, and they put it in a metal trash can and burned it. The plastic part didn't really burn, just the board. They told me they did this to save my soul from the devil.

Later on, they'd tell me that. Later on, Isaac would rediscover his faith in the Church of Latter-day Saints, and Lance would start hanging with drummers, smoking pot and trying harder stuff by the end of the tour, going down that path with the musicians that paved the way. Later on, we'd all grow up, and abandon each other.

But the devil came to us.

It was in the rafters. I saw the black swooping darkness there, while I couldn't sleep. I saw the menacing drift of shadows. In the darkness, walking into the hallways of those big, empty high schools, all the lockers hanging open like some spirit had moved a whole place to abandonment, I felt the tingle in the back of my skull.

It was a bird, up there. A big grackle, swooping from rafter to rafter in the early morning, trapped in the gymnasium, looking down on us with an ugly golden eye like the heart of the Ouija. It made no sound but the flutter of wings. I was the first to see it. People noticed. Nobody did anything.

We made no deal, but we lost, anyway, just opening the line. The good boys that threw away my Ouija board committed an act of theft and vandalism, had opened the line and sinned against me. And me? I had brought them to temptation's door, on a lark. I had let my voice become one with the devil in the board.

I drink alone a lot. I stopped playing music after that summer. I lost the passion for it, and felt like it was time to grow up. I had seen it coming a long way away, but one more summer in the sun did nothing to stoke the old fires in me for the stage and the lights. I drive a delivery truck at night. The city, before it wakes up, the empty streets of the city, with all those shadows and dark places and the ominous rumbling laughter of the crickets and frogs and their night music, all bring me back, and I feel the darkness in me without knowing why. I feel a curse that has no name, no place. It's a low hum, like the rumbling of a song that's just out of tune, a sick feather running over the head of a drum.

I was at my sister's birthday party the other day. She had a Ouija board out, almost as a joke, for people brave enough to drink in her basement. I went down there, and I put my hands on it with whomever came to me, and I moved the planchette. I moved it, and I know I moved it, and we all laughed, and jokingly accused each other, but I moved the planchette and I spoke for the devil.

I did it. I did it and I'll do it again.

WEEGEE WEEGEE, TELL ME DO

ANYA MARTIN

"Weegee, Weegee…"

The Great Marie Cahill's carefully calibrated soprano voice filled every crack and corner of B.F. Keith's Theatre in Indianapolis, Indiana, Stop 87 in this year's circuit, on the afternoon matinee the first Saturday of June 1920. Her generous chest heaved in her ankle-length black and white striped sleeveless dress. Curls of her short blond hair peeked out from under a silver turban, the costume suggesting both a medium and a consummate professional performer. She scanned the audience—every seat taken, not bad for a 54-year-old rather portly matron of the stage. However, without her hourglass body shape and significant girth, she could never have achieved the vocal range that launched her into a music hall sweetheart, a Broadway sensation and now a vaudeville star. Still, she felt the young squeaky-voiced girls of today, all cuteness and curls, scraping at her heels and knew one day not so far off she'd be singing from the other side of the talking board.

"Tell Me Do."

The Great Marie Cahill summoned the high note from deep inside her generous frame and then shimmied her caboose. She gestured upwards with a silver-gloved arm and launched into the rest of the refrain about whether a girl's lover could be true, then leaned back towards the backdrop—a perfect painted giant reproduction of a talking board—sun and moon, YES and NO in each corner, the alphabet arching in two rows across the center, numbers, GOOD BYE at the base. A dark-haired showgirl in a shiny white tutu held a large pear-shaped planchette with a lovely port de bras while doing chaine turns on pointe, pausing to frame "YES" with a lovely arabesque. Her eyes were thickly lined with black shadow and her face and body powdered white to suggest that she was a ghost. The make-up was Marie's idea and one she was quite proud of, thank you very much—just the right balance of spook-show spectacle and sassy sex-appeal.

"…ruler of the nation…"

The Great Marie Cahill was now well into the second stanza about the popularity of the talking board sold officially by the Kennard Novelty Company. Though imitators abounded, Mr. Kennard and his associates regularly challenged all interlopers in the courts. It was probably true that "almost every home" in the country had a Wee-gee, she thought as she sang the words of popular lyricist William Jerome. The tune was quite jumpy with a rhythm that could lend itself to tap-dancing, the latest craze. But she was too old for vigorous onstage athletics—her bones now creaked and her muscles tightened up without her even knowing why. Huzzah also to Harry Von Tilzer, who provided the music to Mr. Jerome's words—another example of his singular ability to cash in on the latest craze.

"…the men who marry girlies…"

***

The Great Marie Cahill enunciated every syllable just as precisely as she did with "Under the Bamboo Tree," her biggest sensation, thought Orlaugh Kelly, seated in the center of the third row. Orlaugh winced and her hands twitched as the second refrain queried whether the supper table should wait for those men who arrive home well beyond suppertime. Joe Kelly, her husband of two years, was rarely on time, and then when he finally arrived teetering from moonshine merriment, he'd complain that the food was "stone cold" and order her to reheat it and then it was taking too long. That was a good night when he didn't just give her a hard punch to the back of her head where it never left a bruise anyone could see. She rubbed her fingers together, concentrating on the tingling sensation at their tips which had started when Joe gave her neck and shoulder a hard twist a few nights ago. Who knew a neck could be so attached to a body part so far away from it? What harm was a little Weegee? Lots when your husband, girlie, didn't like it.

But Orlaugh had never heard him talking in his sleep about a "pearl" to ask the Weegee about—a gift or a girl? And every morning he'd kiss her and say he was sorry before nudging her out of bed to make breakfast. Infernal Irishmen and their whiskey. Just like her Da. Her mother was an angel to put up with it. Her mother was an angel anyway now.

"Tell me."

"Weegee."

"Do."

The piano rippled to a close, then the Great Marie Cahill and her ghost girl sidekick curtsied and bowed. Orlaugh and her friend Daisy jumped to their feet and clapped vigorously, as did most of the audience. After a long standing ovation, the two ladies waved and walked off stage and the curtain dropped. The pianist initiated into a springy entr'acte.

"I bought the sheet music today, for you, at J.W. Pepper with my salesgirl discount," Daisy whispered. "It's the absolute number one song for sheet music sales in the country this week!"

Daisy opened her satchel and pulled out the blue folded paper featuring a jovial man in a tux and a smiling woman in a red dress with their hands on a talking board.

"Jeepers," Orlaugh exclaimed, reading aloud: "The Craze of the Country, the Great Ouija Board!"

"Now, look, your hands are totally shaking, you're so excited," Daisy giggled.

Orlaugh's hands were shaking, but that's because she couldn't get them to stop. She put the sheet music in her lap and sat on her fingers.

The emcee emerged to announce the next act: "Now presenting The Whitman Sisters, Royalty of Negro Vaudeville." The curtain swung up to reveal a black couple in front of a backdrop of giant watermelons. "Bert" Whitman, short for Alberta, a male impersonator, was dressed in a dapper suit with a top hat. "Baby" Alice was an attractive buxom woman in a short dress covered with cascading strands of glittery yellow beads. Bert launched into a jumpy tune about wanting a woman who could shim-sham-shimmy, while "Baby" Alice began a raucous tap routine of wings, pullbacks, and time-steps.

"Let's get Madame Cahill to sign it!" Daisy said, her voice rising above a whisper. "When she hears you sing, you're going to be the next vaudeville star!"

"No, Daisy, I need a lot more practice before I sing anything for a real star like Madame Cahill," Orlaugh protested. At least her fingers had stopped twitching, but they still tingled under the pressure of being jammed between her legs and the cushion.

The Whitman Sisters were well into their act by now, and a gal behind them shushed loudly.

Daisy turned around and hissed sharply in her Daisy way: "I paid my nickel for the show, too. Get back to kissing."

The gal behind wrinkled her nose but her boyfriend, a skinny fellow in a brown tweed suit that looked just a tad like it needed growing into, planted a kiss on her mouth right away, no doubt happy to have any excuse. His "beloved" gave him a little slap but then fell into the smooch, as if the momentary drama was well-rehearsed.

"Come on," Daisy said, rising. Orlaugh's hand sprang out from under her thigh as Daisy reached for it. Orlaugh's other hand grabbed the sheet music. And before she knew it, Daisy had pulled her in front of all the rest of the occupants of their row, some grumbling audibly as the two young women stumbled across their feet. Daisy stepped hard enough on one man's shoe to make him yelp.

At the stage door, Daisy explained to the burly gentleman stationed as security that Orlaugh absolutely must meet "Madame Cahill, s'il vous plait." She had taken two years of French in high school, but Orlaugh suspected that any French person would have cringed at Daisy's pronunciation.

"Orlaugh's mother Patricia O'Brien died of Spanish influenza in the great epidemic of 1918, you see, but before she died, she saw Madame Cahill sing 'Under the Bamboo Tree' on Broadway with Orlaugh, and her Ma, Patricia O'Brien, on her dying bed, declared that Madame Cahill sings like an angel, an angel. Just like Orlaugh sings, and she must make every effort to meet her. And her mother is an angel in Heaven now…"

Daisy could talk her way into any place from a church social to a speakeasy. Meanwhile not just Orlaugh's hands but all of her was shaking with nervousness at meeting one of her favorite vaudeville performers. She counted on the man saying what was likely true—no one was allowed, or at least to wait until the end by the stage door, not while the performance was still going. But instead Orlaugh saw a tear drift down his cheek, and he asked the two girls to write their names down on a card. Then he said he'd go check with Mrs. Cahill as to whether she was up to visitors. He returned a few minutes later to say Mrs. Cahill would see the two young ladies right away if they followed him.

The Great Marie Cahill was a big enough star to have her own dressing room in the very back of the theater. Daisy whispered, "Jeepers" in Orlaugh's ear as they entered and saw the make-up table with a big mirror completely surrounded by round electric lightbulbs. A bouquet of red roses sat on the table, next to several more vases all full of flowers. The Great Marie Cahill was seated in front of it, still dressed in her stage costume except for the turban which sat on a wig head by the mirror. She stood and stretched out a silver satin-gloved hand. She was much shorter than she seemed onstage, very short actually. And yet still larger than life, her hair clipped into a bob and slicked tight around her face, framed with a dainty curl on each side.

***

The Great Marie Cahill was used to having fans request to meet her, but she immediately sensed something delightful about Orlaugh, so pretty and earnest and clearly entranced by meeting a star. The other girl, she could tell, was the ringleader, but she always found quiet girls had more interesting things to say. It just required a little patience and a soft touch to get them to open up.

Lately she rarely received fans so young and eager. Most were older women who remembered seeing her from long ago or older men who didn't mind a little extra on a woman and didn't realize or care that she was married to Mr. Daniel V. Arthur. Some had sussed that Daniel and she had an arrangement that things happen when a couple lives apart so much of the time. She felt a little sad letting them leave disappointed because a dalliance with another man wasn't usually what she was looking for.

The Great Marie Cahill glanced at the card and read both names aloud: "Miss Daisy Hammond and Mrs. Orlaugh Kelly."

"It's pronounced Or-la with the emphasis on la, like singing," Daisy said.

"Apologies for the error, Orlaugh," the Great Marie Cahill said, stretching the second syllable. "It should come as no surprise that laughter is a favorite pastime of mine, but music is my utmost joy. How beautiful that your name evokes singing."

***

Both girls shook her hand, Orlaugh having to concentrate hard to keep her own hand from jerking.

"You have a strong handshake for such a small girl," the Great Marie Cahill commented.

"I'm sorry, I didn't mean to…" Orlaugh began.

"Nonsense," the Great Marie Cahill said. "I believe that force in a woman is an admirable attribute. I hope you employ it to good use."

"Well, I can lift the big pot completely full of stew…"

"Orlaugh's parents took her all the way to New York City in 1917, when she was sixteen, to welcome her brother Sean O'Brien home from the Great War," Daisy broke in. "Her brother Andrew did not make it back, his body never recovered from the trenches of La France. This trip was Orlaugh's only excursion outside of Indiana and her sole experience of the wide, wide world. It happened to coincide with a one-woman show by you, the Great Marie Cahill, in which you sang all your favorites. Even her Ma, usually more enamored with church choirs than popular entertainments, admitted the Great Marie Cahill sang like an angel. Unfortunately her Ma was tough as nails but not as tough as the Spanish influenza. Ever since then Orlaugh has come to see vaudeville with me twice a week, and she goes home and sings in the very hope of someday singing like you, like an angel, for her Ma who is an angel."

***

The Great Marie Cahill was quite taken by the young woman's passionate soliloquy in support of her friend. Though she assumed that Orlaugh probably didn't sing as well as Daisy suggested—the girls who came to her rarely held a candle to her range. "Marie has natural talent," show producers said back when she was young.

"I see you have the sheet music for 'Weegee, Weegee, Tell Me Do,' in your hand," she said.

"If you would be so kind as to sign it, Madame Cahill," Orlaugh replied, her nervousness still palpable, but her hand extended the music boldly forward.

"I'd be most happy to," the Great Marie Cahill replied. "You do know I didn't write the song, though? I only sing it."

"Oh, I've heard all about Tin Pan Alley," Orlaugh said. "I'd love to go there myself sometime."

The Great Marie Cahill chuckled, laid the sheet music down on her make-up table, and signed the front in a flourish of fountain pen atop the heads of the couple contacting the Ouija.

"Okay, now I'd like to hear you sing it," the Great Marie Cahill said.

"What?!" Orlaugh protested, ready to bolt.

Daisy grinned and put her hands together as if ready to clap.

"She's mighty good, Madame Cahill," Daisy added. "Mr. Smith, the choir director, says Orlaugh's a 'natural.'"

"A natural?" the Great Marie Cahill said. "Well, then I must hear you. Do you sing a capella or do we need to find a piano?"

***

"I can sing without accompaniment," Orlaugh said, immediately regretting her admission.

"She's a bit of a Weegee fanatic," Daisy chimed in.

"I know the words to all your songs," Orlaugh said, getting annoyed at her friend's constant banter. And now that she was committed to singing, wanting to get it over as soon as possible.

The Great Marie Cahill seemed to share her desire, gesturing her to begin. Orlaugh began:

"There is a game…"

Her hands soon joined in. First a few claps, then the right slipping to the side, the left going to meet it, a twist and a turn of her arms. Soon her feet were tap-dancing along.

***

Orlaugh's voice was more high-pitched than the Great Marie Cahill, that little girl twang so coming into vogue, but the Great Marie Cahill had to admit by the first refrain of "Weegee, Weegee, Tell Me Do," she was impressed. And the girl had a talent for dancing, too. Not to mention being cute as pie. The Great Marie Cahill wanted to reach out and pinch her.

When Orlaugh reached the end of the song, Daisy erupted into frenzied clapping, but the Great Marie Cahill was silent.

"I'm sorry I'm not very good," Orlaugh apologized.

"Quite the contrary, young lady, you are a natural, just as Mr. Whathisname, your choir director, observed," the Great Marie Cahill declared. "How often do you practice?"

"Every day," Orlaugh said.

***

Suddenly the whole experience had turned around. The Great Marie Cahill's complimentary words echoed in her head like a dream, not possible that she actually uttered them. "After I get home from work at the perfume counter at LS Ayres, I fix supper for my husband Joe. But he's always late, so I play the piano and sing. Or I just sing and dance."

"Do you have any children?" the Great Marie Cahill asked.

"No, none yet," Orlaugh said. "I thought once, but I miscarried."

She didn't say because Joe pushed her and how the blood gushed from inside her and how she never thought it would stop. He was so very sorry, he didn't mean to, the whiskey, never again. Her hands fidgeted as she remembered and then locked away the memory again, her right hand turning the key.

"Well, how does your husband—Joe?—feel about your singing and dancing?" the older woman asked.

"He likes it when I sing in church and when I sing for him, but that's hymns and old popular tunes," Orlaugh said. "He doesn't know I practice vaudeville."

She paused and something inside her got a little braver. Her right index finger and thumb snapped. She pulled that hand behind her back quickly and the motion changed to a flick.

"Daisy is right—my dream has always been to sing and dance in vaudeville," Orlaugh said. "I do come twice a week and watch the shows. Saturday matinee and my day off—usually Wednesday. When

Daisy can't come with me, I come by myself."

"I'm playing Indianapolis for the next week. Why don't you come every day to my hotel room—412 at The Grand. You'll practice, and I'll teach you what I know," the Great Marie Cahill said. "If you work hard and are good enough, I'll see what I can do to get you a place with the chorus girls."

Orlaugh's right hand, now no longer behind her back, reached out for a rose, knocking over the entire vase and breaking it, strewing roses and water all over the sheet music, table, and floor.

"Oh, heavens, I'm so sorry," Orlaugh said. "My hands sometimes just seem to have a will of their own. If you have a towel, I'll clean it all up."

She kneeled onto the floor to gather all the flowers.

"No worries, my dear." The Great Marie Cahill pulled Orlaugh up and then ran her fingers through her hair and glided them across her cheek. Then she took Orlaugh's hands into hers. The hands didn't fidget. Orlaugh felt a pleasant sensation she could not explain.

"It's only roses," the Great Marie Cahill said gently. "I get dozens every day from adoring fans, but it's rare to hear a voice as lovely as yours. I'll get someone to clean this. See you after tomorrow's matinee at 5 p.m. Remember, Room 412, The Grand."

"I am so honored, Madame Cahill," Orlaugh said. Daisy reached for the wet sheet music.

"Looks like the signature is fine, only the bottom half got wet," Daisy exclaimed. "Jeepers, thank you, Madame Cahill. Orlaugh will be there tomorrow. Good-bye!"

She grabbed Orlaugh's hand and pulled her friend out of the room.

***

The Great Marie Cahill didn't have a servant to call. She bent down and picked up the roses, then the bigger shards of glass and brushed the rest into a dustpan with a broom in the corner. She then wiped down the floor with a towel. She looked in the mirror, adjusted her curls, winked at herself. Yes, she still had it.

She wondered if Orlaugh's buttocks were as soft as her cheek.

***

Out on Pennsylvania Avenue, Daisy shook out the sheet music gently.

"It didn't get very wet at all, should dry out just fine," Daisy said. "I knew Madame Cahill would love your singing. I am so excited."

"But how am I going to go see her without Joe finding out," Orlaugh said. "Five o'clock is right before suppertime. And even if she decides I'm good, I can't run off and join vaudeville with a husband to take care of."

"Come on, Joe or vaudeville, it'd be an easy choice for me," Daisy said. "I'm going to get us some ice creams."

Before Orlaugh could protest, Daisy had ducked inside the ice cream parlor.

Daisy couldn't understand how angry Joe got, how it felt to have his fist knock into the back of her head, how her neck ached and her hands tingled and sometimes did stuff she didn't tell them to do.

Her thoughts were cut short by the revolving mechanical beat of an approaching organ grinder in German lederhosen with suspenders and a hat with a feather. His monkey scuttled ahead of him on a leash. Orlaugh knew them well. Everybody who spent any time in downtown Indianapolis did. She bent down and the monkey bowed like a gentleman and took her left index finger to shake it. Her left hand grasped the tiny paw. The poor thing struggled to get loose but she could feel her fingers squeezing its paw tighter and tighter. Shrieking in pain, it dropped the tip cup from its right hand and it jangled as it fell on the pavement. Her hand released. The organ grinder stopped playing and cradled the monkey in his arms.

"I'm so sorry," Orlaugh said, picking up the tip mug and placing a whole nickel inside before she handed it back to the German gentleman. He shuffled away, still holding the frightened monkey.

Daisy walked out of the ice cream parlor and handed her a cone.

"I got you pistachio. It's settled. We have to ask the Weegee," Daisy said as they walked down Pennsylvania licking their cones.

"Ask what?" Orlaugh asked Daisy.

"Whether you should run away from Joe and join vaudeville with the Great Marie Cahill?" Daisy said. "Of course, if the spirits have any sense, they'll say yes."

"I don't think the Weegee answers 'if' questions," Orlaugh said. "Just yes or no or direct questions. Or lets you talk to loved ones."

"Well, let's ask your mother then," Daisy said.

"My ma's in Heaven, she never gave credence to any kind of communicating with the dead," Orlaugh said. "She always thought it was the way to the Devil."

"Well, we have to ask the Weegee," Daisy said. "Because you wouldn't be having this momentous opportunity if it wasn't for the Weegee song."

"If Joe comes home and finds us doing Weegee, he's going to be really angry. He already doesn't like me to have visitors unless I arrange with him in advance."

"He's never home until late, you always say."

Daisy wasn't going to give up. She never gave up. And she was right—Joe never came home early.

"Look! Well, that decides it!" Daisy exclaimed, pointing up at the marquee at the Ritz Theatre which now showed motion pictures.

"NOW PLAYING: Cohn Brothers' Hall Room Boys TELL US OUIJA Starring Neely Edwards and Hugh Fay."

Weegee really was the "ruler of the nation."

***

Orlaugh closed the lace curtains sewn by her grandmother Orlaugh "Mae" O'Brien to block the late afternoon sun, lit several candles, and set them up on the mantel. Then she went into the bedroom and carefully lifted the talking board and planchette from under her lingerie in the second drawer of her dresser where she hid it from Joe. Daisy meanwhile moved the coffee table aside.

The two young women hiked up their skirts and sat cross-legged on the floor, just like they used to when they were little and played parlor games, then Daisy laid the board across their laps. The routine was as familiar as getting dressed in the morning with all the times they'd consulted the board in the past few months. Next, they placed two fingers from each hand—index and middle finger—on the planchette. Orlaugh's numb fingertips tingled when they touched the planchette, much like the time she got an electric shock when plugging in a lamp in the housewares department at L.S. Ayres & Company Department Store where she worked four days a week.

"Let's start with romantic questions, just to get the board warmed up before you ask the important one," Daisy said. "Deep breath. Close your eyes. Open again. Weegee, Weegee, Tell Me, Do. Is Harry true to me?"

The planchette didn't budge at first.

"You're pressing too hard, Orlaugh," Daisy said. "The spirits can't move it if you're applying that much pressure."

With the numbness in her fingers, Orlaugh had no idea she was pressing hard. She almost didn't feel the planchette under her fingers at all. At Daisy's command, however, she sensed them lift a little.

Another minute passed and then the planchette began to glide ever so slowly—at first almost undetectable and then just enough to see the motion. Up over G and H.

Stopped again.

Daisy's eye twitched. Orlaugh could tell she was worried she shouldn't have asked about Harry after all. But the planchette started again, veering left until its circle hovered over "YES."

"Okay, put the planchette back in the center," Daisy said. "I'll ask another question while you pump up your courage. Weegee, Weegee, Tell Me Do. Will Harry pop the question this summer?"

Again the planchette took its time, at least a full minute before it began to coast, slowly at first, then accelerating. Orlaugh's fingers now felt like feathers—did it tickle a little though she didn't feel like laughing? She thought whatever unknown spirit was guiding the planchette seemed nice, even tender, thoughtful and wanting to help. They had done Weegee at least once a week since Daisy got Orlaugh the talking board for Christmas. But it had never felt quite like this. Within three minutes this time, the planchette was again hovering over "YES."

"Okay, your turn!" Daisy chirped, excitement in her voice.

"All right, I'm ready. If I practice with Madame Cahill, will everything turn out all right in the end?"

The planchette didn't move.

And didn't move.

"I shouldn't have asked an 'if' question, should I?" Orlaugh said.

"Hush, what we shouldn't have is a conversation. Maybe the spirit needs to think. You asked it a very serious question."

Orlaugh concentrated silently, trying to recompose the question in her head in case the planchette didn't respond, without revealing how much she was afraid of Joe to Daisy. She did want more than anything in the whole wide world to train under the Great Marie Cahill and run away on the vaudeville circuit. Just like as a little girl she wanted to run away from her drunken father and cruel, teasing brothers, to join the circus. She didn't want to think about the time that Andrew touched her where he shouldn't have. Or that she wasn't sad that the war took him and wished it had taken both her brothers. She hoped Andrew's spirit wasn't the one talking. She knew it wouldn't be Ma because Ma wouldn't leave Heaven. Half of why she married Joe was to get away from Da, after Ma died—not expecting that as soon as she took her wedding vow in the fancy white dress she got on discount at L.S. Ayres, he'd be the same. And everyone said she'd scored with the dashing football champ. High school sweethearts. What possibly could go wrong?

Only everything.

Orlaugh realized her grip had tightened again on the planchette, and eased up until she felt the feather sensation again. At that moment, the planchette started to slide, first so slowly as to be almost imperceptible to the eye but palpable under her fingers.

Up and then right until the circle centered right above the letter H.

Odd. She thought she'd asked a "yes" or "no" question.

The planchette lingered on A, but then jerked right until almost landing on E, so fast that the girls' fingers almost slipped off it. The spirit didn't seem benevolent any more. Orlaugh had never been scared of Weegee before.

Down to N.

Back up to D.

And then down again, slight right. S.

H-A-N-D-S.

Orlaugh felt a sharp pain in both of her hands, which radiated suddenly up her arms. She pulled them abruptly from the board.

The planchette continued to move with just Daisy's fingers on it, down to "Good Bye."

The Weegee was done.

Now that Orlaugh's fingers no longer were on the planchette, the pain receded.

"Well, what do you think that meant?" Daisy asked. "Maybe you're supposed to use your hands more when you sing and dance?"

"I don't know, our hands are on the planchette," Orlaugh said. "Did you feel it? Like something good, then something bad?"

"Oh, Orlaugh, don't be silly," Daisy giggled. "You sound like the Seven Day Adventists warning that old Devil's in the Weegee. I think it means you need to take your life into your hands. You're going to vaudeville and you're going to be a star!"

Orlaugh liked the sound of that. She realized that her hands were no longer numb. Had whatever spirit in the Weegee cured them? If yes, she was grateful. In fact, her arms and neck felt better, too, like all the pain caused by Joe had been erased from her body.

**

Joe worked six days a week at Jimmy Murphy's Auto Repair, which catered regularly to the drivers of the International 500-Mile Sweep-stakes Race, or Indy 500 for short. Last week all he could talk about was winner Gaston Chevrolet getting his car serviced a few weeks before this year's race. On Saturday nights Joe got paid and headed straight to the speakeasy. He kept a change of clothes at work, a fe-dora, suit and dress shoes so he didn't have to come home in between. That was why Orlaugh could sneak out to see a show with Daisy and dared to do the Weegee afterwards. However, he would notice and she'd get a hearty throttle if his socks weren't clean, so while simmer-ing a pot of soup on the stove he'd probably not eat until Sunday lunch, she washed them in the bathroom sink. One sock had a big hole, making her think of the line in the Weegee song about all he wants now is for her to "darn his socks."

Around midnight, Orlaugh had already gone to bed when she heard Joe fumbling with the key at the front door. When the door opened, she heard him trip on the threshold and fall into the coffee table. She always kept the coffee table empty of anything breakable, just magazines, but she thought of the Chinese porcelain vase, bought at Charles Mayer & Company, that Ma gave them as a wedding pres-ent, on the mantel.

"Goddammit!" Joe yelled loudly in the living room, followed by shuffling sounds as he re-found his balance and switched on the elec-tric light. "Orlaugh! Get in here, now!"

Orlaugh jumped out of bed and pulled on her green silk dressing gown. She knew not to tarry when Joe called. The electric light gave just enough illumination to find her way.

The coffee table was ruptured right down its center, shards of frac-tured wood fraying along the fissure. Joe's black fedora lay amidst the wreckage. Joe stood in the center, an unlabeled bottle in one hand and the planchette in another.

"What the Hell is thisssssss?" Joe yelled at her, his voice slurring. "I tripped on it walking in the door."

Orlaugh clearly remembered returning the planchette to her lin-gerie drawer. Her hands, which had been fully under her control all evening, began to twitch again.

Joe bent in her direction, trying to sound like a girl.

"What did you ask the talking board, dumb Dora, if I was a cake-eater? 'Weegee, Weegee, Tell Me Do?' Is my husband cuddling with another doll? Poor, pitiful you."

Orlaugh stood frozen, her hands now bending into fists and unwrapping at lightning speed. She could feel them wanting to slam Joe across the jaw. She concentrated hard to keep them down. Because then he would hit her back, and she wouldn't be strong enough to fight him off. One day she was sure he was going to hit her so hard that it killed her. If she stood very still, maybe he'd just yell at her and then stumble into bed.

"If I divorced you, you know the court wouldn't give you a dime, dearie, because you fool with that Weegee mumbo-jumbo?" Joe said.

He pressed hard on the wood and broke the planchette in half. Then he hurled the two pieces at the mantel, shattering the Chinese porcelain vase, its pieces raining onto the floor.

Joe lunged towards Orlaugh. Reeking of tobacco and bootleg, he rapidly extended his fist, but stopped inches from the side of her head. As he held it there, Orlaugh felt a gush down her leg, heard the putter of liquid on the floor. She winced with humiliation.

Joe exploded in laughter and pulled back his fist. He took a long, deep swig from the bottle in his other hand and continued to the bedroom. Eyes wet with tears, Orlaugh followed and saw him dive sideways facedown on top of the cover. He mumbled into his pillow, then straightened, turned his head and rolled onto his back.

He spoke again. This time the word was clear: "Pearl."

Orlaugh's hands began to spasm. At the end of the Weegee song, the singer asks whether a man bought a woman a present of pearls or is calling out in his sleep to another girl.

"Is it girl? Or is it Pearl?"

She was sure Joe wouldn't buy her pearls. He didn't make that much money and he spent every spare penny on cigarettes and moonshine.

Her hands pulled her towards her now-snoring husband, wrapped around his neck, and squeezed hard.

She was certain he'd wake and his revenge would be swift. He'd beat her to death for sure this time. But even as he tried frantically to loosen her grip, his legs flailing, her hands didn't budge and only tightened their grip. She couldn't let go now even if she wanted to. Her hands wouldn't allow her.

Where did she muster this sudden strength? She knew the brute force of Joe's muscles firsthand from the times he pinned her down or came home so drunk he collapsed on top of her and she couldn't push him off.

Joe's hands moved more slowly and fell back to his sides, his legs no longer twitching.

Orlaugh's hands finally let go. Joe's eyes were wide open and rolled back, but he was dead.

***

Orlaugh went to the bathroom and slipped out of her nightgown, then let her hands take over. They scrubbed her legs with a washcloth, and then used another for her body. They washed her hair in the sink. Once they'd toweled it dry, they took scissors from the jar in the kitchen and clipped it into a bob—just the right length so that it curled in at her cheeks just like the Great Marie Cahill. They applied powder, rouge, eye liner and ruby red lipstick which she'd bought and hidden in her lingerie drawer with the talking board.

Orlaugh's hands dressed her in silk stockings and her prettiest chemise, not the latest style but a light sky-blue that went well with her black Mary Janes. Then they packed her suitcase with only her cutest clothes and all of her lingerie. They didn't forget Ma's brooch that Pa bought her at Carl L. Rost Diamond Merchants on Illinois Street on their twenty-fifth wedding anniversary, nor her grandmother Orlaugh Mae's embroidered handkerchiefs. Her left hand, though, did remove her wedding ring and placed it in an envelope. Wise decision, as she could sell it later if she needed money.

She glanced at the clock—4 a.m. Her left hand turned the knob on the front door, the right hand carrying the suitcase. If it was heavy, Orlaugh couldn't tell—only that she had no problem lifting it. Her right hand set it down and locked the door. The streetcars didn't run this early, so she'd have to walk.

***

The first rays of sunlight were painting the downtown sky when she arrived at the Grand Hotel of Indianapolis. She walked up to the front desk and asked for Room 412.

When the Great Marie Cahill received the early call, she was at first surprised and then intrigued. Opening the door, she found a girl considerably more confident and even lovelier than the shy pretty twig she had met the previous afternoon. Indeed she would never have suspected that the exquisite bob was cut by Orlaugh and not at a fine hair salon.

She motioned Orlaugh inside and invited her to join her in the large bed if she needed a little more sleep. The Great Marie Cahill was only an early riser when travel demanded. The younger woman slipped out of her dress and undergarments as if she slept every night in the "au naturel." The Great Marie Cahill approved, even if she was not herself comfortable with revealing her aging, ample body as Eve in Eden.

The young woman responded favorably when the older woman curled close to her. Orlaugh took the Great Marie Cahill's left hand into hers under the covers. What soft skin, delicate fingers, she thought as Orlaugh's right hand touched her lips and guided them towards her neck.

***

The police didn't discover Joe's body until Friday, ironically when Daisy reported not having heard from her best friend. They arrived at the Grand to arrest Orlaugh on Saturday evening when the two women were packing their suitcases to leave for Chicago in the morning. Orlaugh was excited to perform on stage for her very first time in one of vaudeville's biggest cities as the new sidekick of the Great Marie Cahill, and she'd almost forgotten she'd murdered her husband. Well, it wasn't really her. It was her hands and she couldn't have made them stop, even if she tried.

Orlaugh had never been as happy as in those six days with the Great Marie Cahill, who was frankly stunned upon the officers' arrival. That sweet young woman couldn't have committed such a heinous crime, she protested. However, it occurred to her that Orlaugh hadn't mentioned her husband once since her unexpected arrival at a rather strange early hour almost a week ago.

Orlaugh was in the powder room when the police arrived, and when she didn't open the locked door after considerable knocking and calling, the police broke it down.

Inside they found a pretty young woman with a stylish bob, her own hands wound tightly around her neck. Later the coroner would have to break the poor girl's arms to dislodge the grip and prepare her body for burial.

After Daisy told her side of the story to an earnest young reporter at the *Indianapolis Star*, just about every Indianapolis citizen was talking for weeks about another case of the Weegee driving a young woman mad. The Seventh Day Adventists added Orlaugh's tragic tale to their true tales of the sins of Ouija. The Great Marie Cahill took a short break from the circuit, and then started a new act featuring comedic monologues of gossipy telephone calls.

Sales of the talking board soared.

WHEN THE EVIL DAYS COME NOT

NATHAN CARSON

Paul stood shimmering in the heat on the porch of the old school. Behind its bleached columns loomed the ruins of an aluminum factory piled atop a pocked landscape of bomb craters and red chemical slough.

He heard the tired arc of an airplane split the afternoon sky. Hot wind blew through him, tussling the shiny black hair of a girl perhaps his own age who sat on a nearby bench, oblivious to his presence.

Paul let his gaze follow cracked paint up the imposing front door, then back to the girl hunched over her PhreeFone. He wandered over to stand at her shoulder.

"Coke, curry, sand," he thought he heard her say. One of her fingers glided around the screen. Then her shoulders slumped and she cocked her head, catching Paul with one lazy, bloodshot eye.

"Sometimes," she said, "I can latch a signal when a plane flies overhead. Just long enough to see the headlines. They don't let us read the news here."

Paul stood silent for a moment then replied, "From what I can tell, you're better off not knowing."

The sounds of children enjoying their recess echoed from deep within a nearby crater; laughter and shrieks darted to and fro between blades of browning overgrown schoolyard grass.

She wondered how old he was, so she asked.

He thought about how to answer that. "I turn fifteen on Saturday," Paul said.

The girl sat up straight and ran her fingers through her hair. She felt a rare surge of exhilaration.

"That means you're the same level as me and Signe. It's only been the two of us, so now you'll make three." She stood. "I'm Grace."

She was slender-boned, East Asian-featured, dressed all in black despite the sun. Her only make-up was a raccoon smudge circling her eyes. She pocketed her fone and faced Paul, then sucked self-consciously on her vapuum ring.

Curling clouds exhaled out the corners of her mouth. "I'd offer you a hit, but it's all seconds in here. I get freshies from the janitor. Poor guy is allergic, so he shares his script with the students. I'll make sure he hooks you up, too."

Paul could tell that her one white eye, the one that looked healthy and focused in the right direction, was a lens. Genetically, she was not one of the lucky ones. Not like his family. He wanted to ask what had happened to her other lens, but knew it would be rude.

"Well," she said, "better take you inside and show you around."

Paul watched her open the door and march into the darkness within. Knowing he had no better option, he followed.

***

Whether it was the wind, or its own weight, the door crashed shut behind him, sending a sense of imminence rippling down the entry hall. Farther ahead, Paul could see Grace slipping between long shadows and orange sun haze blurring through the thick, sagging window glass. When she pushed on the tall double doors at corridor's end, a commanding voice boomed through. A voice, Paul feared, he recognized.

Paul sat low on the pew beside Grace, trying to remain out of sight. The dome of the chapel was so high that twitching grey birds roosted in the gilt-peeled rafters. A great robed figure arched over a lectern on a dais, giving his sermon to the scattered children who were uniformly silent and attentive.

"Remember now thy creator in the days of thy youth, when the evil days come not, nor the years draw nigh when thou shalt say I have no pleasure in them…"

Grace used her bad eye to motion Paul toward a copper-mopped girl seated two aisles over. Pale and freckled, she mouthed along with the words of the Father. When the sermon ended, she walked over to greet Grace with a warm hug. Both her eyes looked clean and healthy, as if she'd never worn a lens in her life.

"This is Paul, Signe," Grace said. "He's a freshman, like us."

Signe gave him the same smile, like a flower blooming.

"Wait," Paul said. "How do we know we're the same level? Just because we're the same age, shouldn't I be tested or something?"

Signe giggled. "It doesn't matter, Paul. They teach us as poorly as possible to keep us as long as they can. Graduating from here means casting yourself back into the world. Try not to learn much so that Father Gualdi can protect you too."

At the mention of that name, there came a rapping from the lectern.

"Girls," said Father Gualdi. "Bring the new boy this way."

Paul wasn't ready for this encounter so soon. He slunk down into the pew, twisting his body to conceal his face.

Grace and Signe were baffled. When they turned back toward the dais, they saw Father Gualdi fling his great leather book at Paul with a strength that belied his age.

The book smacked against the wall, so close to Paul it might have flown right through him. The elder's rheumy eyes bulged. A second later the boy rushed out the door.

Crow's feet spread round Father Gualdi's head like a spider web. "Girls, go fetch him for me. Bring him to my office for induction."

Grace stepped between him and the door. "We'll find him. But, Father, may we show Paul around first? There hasn't been a boy in our level as long as I've been here."

"Oh yes," Signe chimed in. "You have all the time in the world, Father. Do let us?" She handed him back the book he had thrown.

Father Gualdi observed them. His skeletal hands clasped the book. "So it is the Crandon boy. Bring him to me, when he is ready. I am nothing if not patient. Run along." Then he smiled, revealing perfect teeth, yellowed with age, false as hope in humanity.

***

"You each have your own room?" Paul asked, marveling.

Signe had decorated her walls with dyed fabrics and rainbow paint. Several gray plastic keyboards from the turn of the century were collecting dust in a corner.

"Of course," she said, while flipping through endless song titles on Grace's fone. She paused for a moment, drew a card from a deck on the windowsill, let it flutter to the rug where Paul and Grace were seated. Face up it showed the Three of Cups. Then she went back to scanning her playlist. She wanted to ask Paul how he and Father Gualdi knew each other, and hoped that the right music would soothe him into sharing.

"Aha," she said, then tapped Play with a severely chewed nail. A racket of music issued from a speaker on a shelf. She began an interpretive dance to its rhythms.

"Are you into music?" Signe asked Paul.

He thought about that. "I was," he said.

"Ask her who this is," said Grace with a lens wink.

Paul complied. "Signe, what are we listening to?"

Signe stopped dancing. "You really don't know? Weren't you just out in the real world? I thought everybody our age listened to T.Y.O.P."

"Sig," Grace said in a teasing voice, "you've only ever been out there on field trips."

Paul said, "I haven't really been paying attention. I used to go to the symphony with my mom and dad…"

Grace grinned. "Hey, that's what I listen to! Classical all the way. Koto, biwa, you know."

Paul observed her ripped, black clothes and nodded.

Signe's music was reaching a crescendo that sounded like amplified babies cooing over a cacophony of horse hooves and fire bells.

Grace took the fone away and paused it. Paul could see the screen. It read, Album: We Know Better / Artist: Ten Year Old Parent.

"Signe," she said. "Please crack a window?"

"It's not that bad," Signe said in protest.

"No," Grace said with a laugh. "I want to introduce Paul to Kokurri."

"Oh, is that what we're doing?" Signe asked, breaking into the grin that seemed to be her most natural state.

Paul saw the music app recede, replaced by a simple graphic of a red Japanese gate. This shrank until anchored near the top of the screen. An array of black letters and numbers appeared, with Yes and No flanking the red torii gate. A gold coin spun up from the center of the screen.

Grace placed her index finger on the coin. Signe joined her. They both looked at Paul expectantly. He followed their lead.

"Kokurri-San, Kokurri-San," said Grace. (*Ah*, Paul thought. *So she wasn't ordering curry after all.*) "Please come." She repeated this several times with the poise of one practiced in the chant.

Wind flapped the curtains. The hair on the girls' hands stood on end.

Grace asked, "Kokkuri-San, are you here?"

The coin began to move around the screen and their fingers followed it. Grace had half-expected Paul to push it himself, as most first-time players did. But though she felt the coin drawn to Yes, none of the motion seemed to come from Paul. As far as she or Signe could feel, Paul wasn't adding any weight whatsoever.

"Whatever you do, Paul," Grace said, "don't let go. If you do, the Kokurri spirit will haunt us forever."

"Don't scare him," Signe said. "It's not dangerous, Paul. Don't worry."

Paul was worried, but not about playing this game.

"Kokkuri-San," Grace continued. "Why has Paul come to us?"

Once more they felt the pull, and their fingers followed the coin from 3 to 2 to 1. Grace looked at Paul inquisitively. He furrowed his brow, trying to fathom possible meanings.

"I think," he said, "maybe the three was my family. Before."

The girls looked at him with concern. Like all their peers, they had both come to the school as orphans.

"It's okay," he said. "They're okay. They're better off than me now. Let's keep playing."

Grace implored him, "Go ahead. Ask the spirit a question."

"Like what? I don't even know what kind of a spirit this is?"

Signe leaned in. "Kokurri," she said, "is part fox, part dog, and part raccoon. He is cunning and faithful. But he can also be a trickster."

"Ask him," Grace said, "when you will die. I do it all the time. Say, 'Kokurri-San, when is the date of my death?'"

Paul really couldn't see the harm in that. "Kokurri-San," he began, "when is the date of my death?"

The coin began to move again, spinning abruptly from 7 to 2 to 4. Paul snapped his finger off the fone. Grace screeched.

"Paul!" she cried. "Put your finger back! Kokurri-San! We are so, so sorry!"

The curtains fluttered again in reverse and the window slammed shut, breaking the old glass.

"What is it?" Signe asked. "What just happened?"

The fone screen burned with jagged digital flames. A tear dropped from Grace's bad eye.

Paul whispered somberly, "Today is Thursday, July twenty-second. The twenty-fourth is on Saturday."

***

"You can't really believe that, Paul?" Signe looked at him like he was an animal wounded in the street. "Kokurri is just a game. An app!"

Grace just shook her head and stared at the shards of glass on the tiled floor.

"You're wrong," Paul said. "July twenty-four is the date. On Saturday, I will be dead. Sorry to trouble you both with this. I'm going to find my room now."

The girls sat in silence as he walked toward the door.

"Paul?" Signe said. He stopped to hear her out. "What if we can get a second opinion? There are other powers besides Kokurri."

He said, "If it makes you feel better, sure. But it won't change anything. Good night." And he was gone.

***

Paul wasn't at breakfast. The girls ate their plankton waffles in silence. When they'd finished their powdered drinks, they dumped their trays and sought out Father Gualdi.

Eventually they found him in the library. He was the oldest person either girl had seen or even heard of outside storybooks. Veins wove a story through his pale paper skin. White hairs thick as quills sprouted where they chose. But beneath the school roof, his strength and authority were written in blood.

"Father," Grace asked. "If someone thinks they're going to die, like really soon, what should they do?"

"This person must have faith," he said without looking up from his reading. "Utter faith. Works of the law will justify nothing. But death is a blessing. Neither eternal life, nor damnation are fates one should willingly choose to suffer." He then dismissed the girls and resumed his study.

***

Paul was alone on the porch in that dusty light, staring into the orange morning sun. They could tell from his fatalistic expression that nothing had changed in his mind.

"I brought you a waffle," Signe said.

Paul eyed the blue-green wedge. "I'm not hungry," he replied. "Happy Friday the twenty-third."

Grace winced like she'd been kicked in the stomach.

"We just spoke with Father Gualdi," she said.

Paul squinted. "I wish you hadn't."

Grace looked even sadder. "He's a hundred and thirty-two. And very wise."

Paul laughed quietly. "He's been a hundred and thirty-two for about three hundred years."

Grace looked down and scraped one of her feet against the other. "That's not very nice."

"Okay you two grimbears," Signe said, trying to resume her usual demeanor. "There's someone up the street we need to visit right now. Follow me, please." They did.

Potholes perforated the road like model train versions of the bomb craters in the fields beside. Beyond school property, all the other houses and buildings were boarded up, quietly becoming part of the disused landscape.

"I can't believe places like this still exist," said Paul. "Where I grew up, it's one long strip mall connecting all the cities together."

"They know that none of us would stay if there was anywhere to run," said Grace.

"Not much farther now," said Signe. "There it is, up on that little hill."

Around a broken elbow of road stood a narrow concrete

tombstone of a building. It seemed sturdy, though its façade ran rampant with dun moss and decay.

"You've never taken me here or talked about this place before," said Grace.

Signe shrugged. "We all have secrets. Right, Paul?"

"You could say that again," he replied.

She opened her mouth to do just that, but stopped when the screen door of the concrete building swung open in the hot breeze. It slammed shut just as quickly while Signe and her shadow ascended the warped wooden stairs. She peered through a dark window, leaving a clean spot where her nose touched dust. The sign above the door read *Howard's Antiques & Collectibles.*

She turned back to Grace and Paul. "He's not here. But I know how to get in."

Grace reached up and wiped the grime off Signe's nose with her fingertip. Signe giggled and started shimmying up the drainpipe to the awning. Grace and Paul climbed up after her. They were absolutely exposed, but no one was around to see them.

The second story window wasn't locked. They piled through it into a dark, cluttered room. Cobwebbed lampshades overflowed from a rusted shopping cart, which seemed weirdly out of place on the second story. Grace used her fone as a flashlight and Signe's silhouette led them deeper into the old store. The hallway floor, walls and ceiling were covered with posters for films and videogames and soft drinks that their grandparents might have recognized. None of the kids could understand society's former fascinations with sasquatches and gyrocopters, thigh-high vinyl boots and meat-flavored kombucha. At some point now long past, the world really had gone mad.

In front of them was a door with an amber frosted window that glinted like carp scales in the cold fone-light. Beyond it was a deep closet with a dangling pull-string for the single exposed light bulb. Signe yanked it on.

"Ack!" Grace cried out, as her lens dilated gray. Her bad eye shut a split second later. "Warn me next time?" She clicked off her fone.

"Sorry," Signe said. "Now, where is it? Hmm." She was dragging her finger across shelves full of splitting cardboard-boxed games stacked precariously in no apparent order.

"Aha! Grace, reach up there? You're taller than me. That really really old one that says Parker Brothers on it." Grace stood on tiptoe and plucked it from the stack. A cascade of games came down in a rain of counters and spinners and dice, prismatic money, miniature metal knives and a tiny plastic noose.

"Shit. Sorry," Grace said.

Signe knelt down and picked up the box. "It's okay. There's only two things in here that we need." She cradled the package in her arms and pulled the string again, leaving them once more standing in darkness.

***

Signe led them down to the main floor and set the box on a small angular table with a tag that read, *Early aughts Ikea $4999.99*. She drew up three rusting chrome barstools and lifted off the lid. Inside the box was a board that unfolded into something like the Kokurri mat, but altogether more exotic, because it was printed on a large tan sticker. Hello and Goodbye, letters and numbers square-danced in a font that looked positively medieval to Grace and Paul and Signe.

"It's beautiful," Grace said.

"Where's the coin?" Paul asked.

"There's no coin," Signe said. "Just this thing. I don't remember what it's called." She placed the planchette on the board and lit tall candles with an old book of matches she found in an ashtray shaped like MexiCanada. "Grace, draw the shades," she said. "We don't need any open doors or windows to talk to these spirits."

Grace walked over to the window and gasped. Through it, she saw a man standing on the porch watching them.

***

"Mr. Howard!" Signe cried in excitement. She ran to the door to greet him as he wiggled his key in the lock. He was handsome and looked to be about thirty, but still accepted Signe's prolonged kiss with ease. It was clear the two had spent quality time together.

"I see you brought some friends this time," he said.

"Mr. Howard, this is Grace, who I've told you about. And Paul, who I haven't. He's new. We came here to help him."

Howard was drawn immediately to the table, where he moved the dripping candles to a safe distance from the Ouija. "Careful, Sig. This one is vintage."

"That's how I know it works," she said. "I'm glad you're here. You're way better at this than I am. Paul here got some bad advice from Kokurri. Now he thinks he's going to die tomorrow."

Howard smiled. "Nobody's dying tomorrow. Paul, come sit across from me. Place your hands on the planchette." Howard sat and showed him how, like a mirror reflection of Paul if he was fully grown and dressed like a character in an ancient black and white movie.

"Girls," Howard said. "Please join hands with each other. Make a circle and turn slowly." As they spun, the candle flames began to blur into a ring of fire. In the corners of the room, mannequins and dress form torsos seemed to leap into dance, etheric bodies painted in bands of variegated light.

"I call upon the spirits," Howard said. "To tell us, on what day our friend Paul will pass from this earthly plane."

The planchette began to slide slowly, then gained speed. At first it swirled in a curve, the shape of a wave from an ancient Asian scroll. Then it lingered briefly on 7, 2, 4, and F. By the time it had rested on Goodbye, Paul had run right out of the house. None of the three remaining had heard the front door open or close.

Howard blew out the candles, carefully boxed up the game, and turned on a few colored lamps. "So," he said. "What do you suppose that meant to Paul?"

Grace and Signe's bodies had stopped spinning, but their minds were still in motion.

"Tomorrow is July twenty-fourth," Grace said. "Just like Kokurri said."

"But then, what is the F?" Signe asked.

"I should think," said Mr. Howard, "it stands for the day of the week."

"But tomorrow is Saturday," Signe said.

Mr. Howard nodded. "Correct. But last year, it was on a Friday."

***

"I don't get it," Grace said, absently setting her fone on the table and picking up the planchette.

Signe sat on Mr. Howard's lap. He put his arms around her in comfort.

"I think maybe I do," Signe said.

Howard squeezed her a bit more. "Have either of you actually touched Paul?" Both shook their heads. "I can attest, he didn't put any weight on the planchette. But it moved nonetheless."

Grace peered at Howard through the planchette's round window with her lens eye. "But why," she asked, "would a ghost come to a school for orphans?"

"Perhaps," Howard suggested, "he has unfinished business. I've lived a long time, my dear. Genetics are definitely on the side of my family. But mine is not the only family with such traits."

"This is nuts," Grace said. "I'm going after him." She left out the front door and shut it behind her.

"So much for having a boy in freshman years," Signe said.

"Well, let's not give up on him just yet," Howard said with a chuckle. "Have you considered calling his parents?"

Signe reached for the fone that Grace, in her haste, had left on the table. "I guess it never occurred to me that he had any. Nobody else around here does."

***

Paul ran all the way back to the school. He knew that making friends with living girls would only make this harder. But they were a nice distraction, and he wasn't anxious to confront Father Gualdi on his own. So he hid himself in Grace's room and got to thinking. Much sooner than he expected, she came back, alone.

She stood in silence for a moment. Paul was still hidden from view. Grace then pulled off the gauzy black top she wore over her bra and began riffling through the drawers of her bureau. Paul stepped up behind her, as he had on the porch the day before. "What are those?" he asked.

Grace shrieked and jumped at the same time, clawing her hands right through Paul. For an instant, it felt like she'd attacked a dust devil. Her fingers stung and her knuckles ached. Then the sensation passed, and she was standing face to face with the ghost of Paul, her eye and lens wide as her mouth. He was still looking in the open drawer. It was filled with a rat's nest of twisted black wires.

"Those," she said in a shaking voice, "are the power cables from all of Signe's keyboards. I steal them when she's not looking. Can't stand the awful sounds she makes with those things. I guess now I know where she keeps getting replacements." She dug her hand into the mess. "Better make room for one more tomorrow."

Paul smiled. "After hearing what kind of music she listens to, I think you're doing the world a favor." Grace grinned back, though she was still unnerved by the whole experience.

"Is it true what you said about Father Gualdi?" she asked.

Paul walked over and sat on her bed. She noticed that he didn't make an impression on the covers, like he was the weight of a feather or less. "Well," he said, "I couldn't tell you exactly. But yes, he's much older than he lets on. And pretty much impossible to kill."

"Why," she asked, "would you want to kill him?" Of course, Grace didn't have the rapport with Father Gualdi that Signe did. But then, Signe had been in the orphanage a much longer time; she'd never known her parents. Five years on, Grace still felt betrayed by the world for taking hers.

Paul pursed his lips as if that could help him think. "An eye for an eye," he said without realizing what a poor choice of words that was. "Gualdi has lived a long time, but he still ages, slowly. My father's a geneticist. They've known each other since way before I was born…"

***

Mr. Howard entered his temporary signal code into Grace's fone, then handed the device to Signe. She looked up at him and asked, "Now what?"

"Well," he said, "you know Paul's full name, right? And a date he considers fairly important. Why not search those terms and see what comes up?"

In moments she'd found the obituary.

***

"My father told me that he was trying to help everyone in the world live as long as Father Gualdi, and other families like ours. Of course I believed him. But now I'm starting to wonder. Anyway, I guess Gualdi wanted to look young again. He kept calling it an *elixir*. Dad laughed at that. 'It's a *formula*, Gualdi,' he'd say."

"So then how did you," Grace started, "I mean, when did you…?"

Paul nodded. "July twenty-fourth is my birthday. I don't know why Gualdi was invited. It happened a year ago. My father had prepared the formula. It…didn't make me younger. Though I guess I won't really be aging anymore, right? So maybe my dad is a genius, after all."

***

The first several calls Signe made were dead ends. But this time, someone answered.

"Pinot Genetic Research Institute Systems," said the automated voice.

"Hello," Signe stammered, nervous. "I'm looking for Dr. Saul Crandon." His name had arisen repeatedly during her searches. Recent photos all revealed his tragic loss. In fact, the photos from the last year were the only ones that showed signs of him aging at all. Crandon seemed to have been a handsome, healthy man since before photography had been invented.

"I'm afraid," the voice responded, "Dr. Crandon was fired nearly a year ago. After the unfortunate death of his son."

***

"But why did you drink it if it wasn't for you?" Grace asked.

"It wasn't my idea," Paul said. "Gualdi tricked me into drinking it. I don't know why it was toxic. I guess Gualdi had a suspicion, though. And he knew it would be worse for my family if I were killed by something my own father had made. If I could go back and do it differently, I would."

Grace pulled a night shift over her head, then closed all the drawers in her bureau. She saw herself in the mirror, alone in the room. But when she turned around, Paul still sat on her bed.

"I guess I was kind of hoping," Paul said, "that seeing me now would scare him to death. Seems like it's not gonna to be that easy."

"What happens if you just leave him alone?" It was freaky to her that she could see Paul through her lens but not in her mirror. What was the difference between a ghost and a vampire again, she wondered? Something about teeth?

"I can't do that," Paul said. "Not sure I can explain it to you, but I need to end it tomorrow. Otherwise, I'll be stuck."

Grace was feeling exhausted by all of this. She willed herself to sit on the bed beside him. "I'll help you," she said, "however I can."

Paul smiled. "Thank you, Grace. Could I stay with you tonight? Please? I seem to think more clearly when I'm not alone."

She slid under the covers and he lay down beside, wrapping a weightless arm around her.

***

In the morning Grace awoke to a clap of thunder. She reached groggily for her fone, then remembered that she'd left it at Howard's shop. Next she recalled Paul. He was gone too.

On examination, Signe's bed hadn't been slept in, either.

***

Paul entered Father Gualdi's private chamber.

"You are quite punctual, Mr. Crandon," came Gualdi's rasping voice from behind his desk. He stood, making an imposing figure. Between thumb and forefinger, he gripped the lens he'd taken from Grace five years prior, and slipped it over one deeply cataracted eye. His sinister yellow smile glowed dully in the ochre morning light. "And, may I add, happy birthday?"

***

Grace finally found Signe on the porch of the school. Her mussed red hair and damp clothes made it look like she'd been up all night. But while Grace was anxious and scared, Signe seemed both hopeful and satisfied. "We found him," she said, then returned Grace's fone to her. Grace took it and tapped the screen. A series of calls had been made to strange numbers. Just as she was going to ask who the calls were to, a sleek black car arrived, steaming in the pissing rain.

***

"Before we do this," Paul said, "I want to know why you made me drink it. The formula was for you. Aren't you sick of looking like a corpse? How long til you just crumble into worm food?"

Father Gualdi laughed, though it sounded more like a hiss. The smell of his primeval flesh permeated the room.

"My son, I have shed the selfish desire for youth. Your father has troubled me for decades. If you only knew how many lovers of mine he has stolen, how many times he forced me to change cities and names. I curse the day our paths first crossed. My lot has been to serve the lord above. Saul Crandon seems to take breath solely to see me writhe."

"Then why," Paul asked, "did you come to us? Why didn't you stay away?"

"Your father fooled me one last time with his false promises. I live, yet as you can so clearly see, my body ages and falters. Your father, so clever, so fortunate; he has eluded both death and decay. He promised to share this gift with me. And I trusted him. But wisely, I did not trust him overmuch.

"Have you not guessed, young Crandon? How sad that your progenitor did not reveal to you the secret: that black elixir prepared for me was no miracle—just another of your wretched family's poisons. Had it been the fountain of youth, I'd be damned before I'd drink from your father's chalice now. But you were all too eager."

Paul was aghast. "So you actually want to keep aging?"

"No," Gualdi replied. "I wish to die. But your father's 'formula' would have accomplished nothing. My quandary is far more metaphysical. I had hoped that stealing the pleasure of thy youth would ruin Saul Crandon and appease my need for revenge. Surely, no price could be placed on seeing your mother's face at the funeral."

"I remember," Paul whispered.

"But still," Gualdi said with finality, "though I risk my immortal soul in the process, I find that I cannot bear to perish while your line continues."

"Well," Paul said, "my father doesn't know that I'm here. Seems like you failed."

Father Gualdi fanned his robes like black wings and stepped around his desk toward the office door, a ceremonial dagger clutched in his claw-like hand. "I beg to differ."

Then came a knock. Gualdi opened the door. Paul couldn't see beyond the Father's robes; but he heard his own father's voice cry his name.

GRIEF

TIFFANY SCANDAL

"Sometimes when I close my eyes, I can still see his body."

Marcy stared at her coffee. A bleak nothing. Decaf. She had switched over because she drank more when she was anxious and the caffeine was making it worse. Her head was already fogged enough with grief. She looked up at the lights. She hated crying in public.

"My boy, he was so young…"

The warmth of a hand covered hers. Across the table from her sat an elderly man, smiling, warm, sympathetic. A grief counselor who met people in public and helped them process feelings over the loss of loved ones. Marcy sniffled, lips quivering. She couldn't make eye contact; it'd make the crying worse. So she looked down or at his mouth as it spoke or into her lap as she pretended to listen. "I failed him. What does this say of me, as a mother?"

The counselor's smile didn't waver. He tapped on her hand and shook his head. "Marcy, you have to understand that you did what you could for your little boy. You did everything right."

Everything. Right…

"The rest we have no power over."

After her boy Hunter fell ill, everything happened too quickly to

67

sink in. One day he was playing in the front yard, the next he was in a hospital bed with a doctor speculating it could be a growth in his pancreas causing him to throw up so much. There hadn't been any signs. No visible journey. Overnight he went from a hungry boy eating his dinner to not even being able to keep down water. He'd needed a transfusion just to stabilize. He'd looked so weak in the bed.

Money had been tight, but she hadn't hesitated to opt for any chance offered. Even if it only meant just a little more time. There was no backup plan, no regard for piling debt. But none of that mattered: she would do anything to make her baby boy healthy again.

And a few weeks after the surgery, he died.

After his release from the hospital, Marcy had taken leave from work to watch over Hunter. She cooked and cleaned and budgeted, and did whatever she could to keep him comfortable. They were glad to have him home. They wanted to see him smile, to see him happy. Marcy and her partner David joked and played with him. Watched movies. Let him eat whatever he wanted. But Marcy and David would fight after Hunter went to sleep. The fighting started within the first week of his illness. At times she'd get so angry with David she'd want to just leave and take Hunter with her. But she couldn't leave; not now. Not while Hunter was sick. So she started smoking and in the night calm of outside air she'd imagine cancer cells replicating in her lungs.

Then one night, while David was at work, Marcy had tucked in Hunter. He had seemed less energetic that day, but the doctor had told them to expect that after the procedures he'd been through. Sitting on the side of his bed, she brushed his dark brown hair off of his forehead and kissed him goodnight.

"Gross," Hunter fussed.

"Turd." Marcy messed up his hair and secured the stuffed pterodactyl under his arm.

Then she told him to get some sleep and turned off the lights.

The house was quiet, calm. She went outside to smoke and collect her thoughts.

How's Hunter? David texted.

Fine. I just tucked him in for the night.

Okay. If you need me to leave work early, just let me know.

Even though David wasn't the best partner, he was at least a really good father, and Hunter needed that right now. People who loved him.

In the distance, Marcy noticed a shooting star. A glow tearing through the night sky. Something felt heavy inside of her body. She looked back toward the house and whispered Hunter's name. She quickly snubbed out her cigarette and ran back inside to check on her boy.

"Hunter! Hunter!"

He didn't respond at first, but his body was still warm. Marcy took him in her arms and shook him.

"Hunter!"

When he groggily opened his eyes, Marcy felt a huge wave of relief.

"Whaaattt?"

"Nothing, honey. I just wanted to make sure you were okay."

Hunter nodded his head and laid back down.

Marcy chuckled. She tucked him back in and left the room.

The dread never left her. But rather than check on her son every five minutes, she opted to just keep busy around the house. Knowing David would be home soon, she cracked open a bottle of wine and waited for him on the couch amidst the freshly clean home.

Keys in the lock, Mercy stood up and smiled, ready to hand him a glass of wine. He looked tired.

"You're drinking?"

Not even a hello.

"I just opened this. Figured it'd be nice to unwind."

"Unwind? You're not even working. What is there to unwind?"

"David, you don't have to be so mean. I just thought we could enjoy a glass together. Something nice, you know?"

David walked past her and didn't take the glass she offered.

Marcy could already feel like she was about to start crying again, so she just went toward Hunter's room. If anything, she'd sleep there and keep watch over her boy.

In the doorway, she dropped the glass of wine.

Hunter was facedown on the floor. Like he had crawled out of bed and was making his way to the door before he fell. His green footie pajamas made him look like a little tyrannosaurus rex. The material looked so soft in the light.

"Hunter?"

"What's going on?"

David ran up to Hunter's room and pushed past Marcy. He picked up Hunter and checked him.

"He's not breathing."

Marcy couldn't move. Her breath caught in her throat.

"Call 9-1-1!"

"Wha-wha…"

David got up and ran past Marcy again, bumping her into the doorframe this time.

"For christ's sake, Marcy. Do something," he scolded as he ran past. "Yes, we need an ambulance…my son. He's not responsive. Hurry!"

He pushed past her again and shoved his phone into her hands. "Was that so difficult?" He turned Hunter over and started administering CPR.

Hunter, her six-year-old boy. He looked so small next to his father.

She fixated on the pterodactyl that was next to her little boy. Her movements felt slow, blurred. She was on her knees, hugging the dinosaur, staring at Hunter's little hand.

"Marcy! Open the fucking door!" David yelling in front of her.

Marcy just looked at him. His words seemed foreign. She rolled to sit on the floor, still reeling from everything that'd happened.

David ran out of the room again. He returned with paramedics. They surrounded Hunter and tried to revive him.

"He already…" She pointed at David but couldn't produce the rest of the words to finish her sentence.

David was talking to the paramedics. Answering questions. But she couldn't focus on the words they were saying.

"Call it."

Marcy noticed the blue gloves not doing anything.

"Is-is he go-going to be okay?" That's when she looked at Hunter's face. He looked so peaceful. Like a little angel. She clutched the dinosaur tighter.

The paramedic looked at his partner. "Ma'am, I'm sorry to say, but your son is dead."

"D-d-dead? No…"

"Yes, a coroner will be here for the body. It's best not to try to move it."

"No. No, Hunter is going to be okay. He had all the surgeries and treatments. The doctor said…"

"I'm very sorry for your loss."

"But he's only six." At that point, Marcy started bawling. David got up and hugged her. She buried her face into his chest. "He's only six."

And just like that, their little boy was gone. Her little boy.

***

Everything hurt. Time became a foreign concept. The days bled into nights, into weeks, into months. After the funeral, the house stayed quiet, felt empty, became filthy. David started drinking vodka directly from the bottle and constantly toasted the ghost of a child that never developed into a friend. Marcy smoked regularly now. Started smoking inside of the house because her boy was dead and nothing mattered anymore. Neither cared about the effect on the other. On the couch together, with the television off, David asked, "Are you hungry?"

"Not really."

"Me either." He nodded and stared at the blank screen.

"It's not fair."

"What?"

"Life." She took a drag from her cigarette. "I think about him more than I think about my mother. It's like his death being so immediate makes her death seem further away. Not gone, just more distant, less significant. I'm afraid of losing him like that. I don't want to lose him."

"I wish I could just talk to him." The drag of his speech more noticeable now. He was drunker than usual, but had gotten good at masking it. "I miss him. He was a good boy."

Marcy tapped ash into a Coke can. "I feel him sometimes, or the memory of him."

"I wish I could hear him snore."

"I wish I could hear him laugh."

"I wish I could just, I don't know, talk to him or something and tell him how much I love him."

"We have a Ouija board." Marcy used to use play with Ouija boards all the time when she was younger. Although it had always been with friends for fun, she did believe in the board's power to communicate with the dead.

"Huh?"

"In the basement."

Before David could say anything else, Marcy got up to look for the board. The bulb over the staircase was burnt out, so she blindly navigated her way down the stairs and walked face first into a cobweb. She screamed, flinched, and fell down the remaining five steps. She landed with a heavy thud and felt the silence that followed swallow her. She looked toward the door she came from, relieved she didn't fall from the top of the stairs. She dusted herself off, fumbled for the light switch, and started digging through musty boxes full of forgotten objects. In one box, she found unframed pictures. Her and David when they were young and happy.

The cat that ran away shortly after they moved into their home. Baby Hunter. Photos that should've been in an album, but were instead recklessly abandoned. She continued to flip through photos and stumbled across her favorite picture of Hunter. There he was, missing front teeth, holding his pterodactyl. That was when Hunter said he hoped the tooth fairy would leave him $1,000 so he could buy his very own dinosaur. The next day, the tooth fairy disappointed him by only leaving a quarter and a brand-new toothbrush. David told Hunter they should form a child's union, and together they built placards to protest against the tooth fairy's wage theft. Marcy wished she had taken a photo of that.

"You alive?" David shouted from the couch.

Marcy rolled her eyes. She fell a while ago, and it *just* occurred to him to check on her? She scanned the rest of the basement and noted the Ouija board on top of the box she was sitting next to.

"Right in front of me," she whispered to herself.

She tucked the pictures under her arm and picked up the dusty game box to take back upstairs.

"You want to try this?"

David chuckled.

"What's he gonna say? The kid barely learned how to read and write." David took a deep breath. Marcy could tell he was about to cry.

She swiped everything off the coffee table and took the board out of the box. Empty takeout boxes, cans, bottles, cigarette cartons flew to the ground. She put the stack of photos on the table next to the board, with the image of Hunter's toothless grin right on top. Planchette on the board, Marcy sat ready with her fingertips ready to channel. David just sat on the couch.

"Come on," Marcy urged David.

He shook his head but reluctantly got up. He mimicked what Marcy was doing.

They both stared at the board and said nothing.

"What now?"

"Uh, I guess we say something. Umm." She cleared her throat. "Uh, hey. Umm. We'd like to communicate with our son. Hunter. Hunter, are you there?"

Nothing happened.

David took his fingertips off of the planchette and dropped them at his side. "This is stupid."

"Maybe we just need to give it more time?"

David opened a bottle of vodka and took a swig.

"No, I'm done. That…that game…it's not…" David started crying.

Marcy walked over to him and put her hand on his shoulder.

"That's not my son." He grabbed the planchette off the board and flung it across the room. Face red, tears streaming down his face, he let his weight fall back into the couch. He looked completely defeated. "I miss him. So much."

"I miss him, too."

She hugged David. He patted her back, which made everything feel worse. Made her feel extra alone. Even though he never outright said it, she felt he believed she was responsible. And maybe she was? She was home when it happened. Maybe if she would've just stayed by Hunter's side the whole time, she would've been able to prevent his death. Even though the coroner and the doctor both said that the cancer was just too aggressive and nothing else could've been done, maybe she could've noticed something was wrong while he was sleeping and rushed him to the hospital in time and the doctors would've treated him and he would've pulled through and he would be okay. He would be alive right now, telling Marcy and David about random facts he learned at school and things about dinosaurs and how monster trucks and astronauts are cool. He would be alive, and Marcy could scoop him up and give him kisses all over his face and he would kick and giggle and tell her that she was gross, but then he'd turn around to hug her and tell her that he loved her. Hunter. Her little boy.

It hurt to think his name.

"I'm sorry."

"What?"

"I'm sorry. For everything."

David looked at her. For the first time in a long time, it felt like he was finally looking at her.

"If I would've just stayed at his side the whole time, maybe… maybe I could've stopped it."

"What?"

"His…his death."

David stared at the floor.

"Since Hunter got sick, any time I left his side, I expected every text, every phone to tell me that he died. That day, I thought about calling out. I looked at him just before I left and it was like I knew. And because I wanted so much to be wrong, I played it cool and just said *see you later, kiddo.* That's it. *See you later.*"

David wiped tears from his face.

"More than anything, I wish I would've called out. And we could've spent the day with him. Watched all of his favorite movies. Ordered, like, ten pizzas and…"

"Let him eat all the candy he wanted."

David chuckled. "Yeah. And I would've loved to hug him and tell him that I loved him very much. God, I wish I could've told him that I was proud of him." He picked up Hunter's photo from the coffee table. "My boy. He was my boy."

"We thought we'd have more time with him."

"Yeah." He stood up.

"David?"

"Yeah?"

"You were a great father."

He nodded and walked away.

***

Nights had been rough since Hunter's passing. Marcy tossed and turned all night, and any dreams she remembered were usually nightmares. One night she dreamt that Hunter was still alive and when she went to hug him, he tore into her neck like a vampire. Another night, she dreamt that she took him to an amusement park but he was so excited and kept running away from her. Every time she tried to keep up, more and more people would just get in the way until she lost sight of him completely. Other times, she'd just wake up crying, not remembering the dream, but figuring it was awful anyway like her son being a monster or her constant failure to be a good mother. She had started going to support groups, seeing grief counselors, trying to talk to anyone that wasn't David because he had grown so detached that sometimes talking to him felt like talking to a wall and any day he would present her with divorce papers but that's a whole other issue she didn't want to think about right now because her son was dead and she would give anything to have him be alive again, even for just one minute so she could hug him and tell him that she loves him.

Lying in bed, Marcy stared at the ceiling. Tears in her eyes, she whispered all the things she wished she could say to Hunter one more time. She heard rapid footsteps coming toward her bedroom door. She wanted to sit up and look, but her body was paralyzed. Was someone in her home? David was snoring on the other side of the bed, so who could be in her house at this time of night? She felt weight pounce on the bed and crawl along her side. Her heart was racing. A cold sweat beading at her brow. Finally feeling the ability to slightly move her head, she looked down and saw the shadow rushing toward her. Just as she was about to scream, the moonlight shone on Hunter's sweet face. His grin with missing teeth inches from her face.

"Mommy!"

"Hunter?"

And he hugged her. His little body, squeezing her as hard as he could.

"Hunter?"

"Yes, Mommy?"

"Wha?" David, still groggy from sleep, but not moving.

"Hunter. Hunter's here."

David sat up but stared at the doorway.

Marcy squeezed Hunter. "I've missed you so much. My baby boy."

"I know, Mommy. It's okay."

"You're here. I can't believe you're here." Marcy started crying.

"I heard you and Daddy earlier."

"When?"

"Earlier. But when I tried to talk to you guys, no one was there."

"The Ouija board? It worked?"

Hunter shrugged in her arms.

She thought about the board. David threw the planchette when he got upset. So if Hunter did try to communicate with them, he couldn't because the planchette was not on the board. But a channel for communication had been been opened.

Marcy tensed.

The channel that was opened was never properly closed.

"Hunter, not that I'm not glad to see you, but how are you here right now?"

Hunter pointed to the dark doorway. "The scary man."

Marcy looked at the doorway and saw something move in the shadows. She hugged Hunter closer, but her arms moved through air and landed on her own body. Hunter was gone. David jumped up and charged through the doorway with the baseball bat he kept by the bed. There was a loud crash and he screamed, then silence.

Marcy stayed in bed, hearing only her own breath, clutching the blankets close to her chest.

"David? You alive?"

SPIN THE THROTTLE

DAVID JAMES KEATON

To play their games, they used the first bottle of whiskey they'd all drained together, back when the fire truck first rolled out. They'd passed it around their circle and then tossed it into a corner of the pool, forgotten. But now this empty bottle of Jim Beam Devil's Cut bourbon refused to cease spinning, and though no one was into the party games as much anymore, the clear violation of the laws of physics got to Beth, who couldn't bear the scrutiny if it stopped to point at her. So she seized it from the waves, and then screwed some sort of tiny message into its neck and tossed it out into the night. Reeves made a half-hearted slap to intercept it, but he was way too far gone by now. They all heard the bottle shatter on the road, message lost.

Their party had been going for at least seven hours, though it was hard to be certain. A dozen of them were crammed and shivering in a hot tub in the back of a 1955 American LaFrance Series 700 pumper that had been haphazardly Dr. Moreau'd into a garish party wagon, one of those ancient fire trucks with a pug nose for a cab and more than a passing resemblance to the hippy buses popularized in the psychedelic '60s, but now decked out with speakers, Christmas lights, and American flags. They'd started out in good spirits, but sometime around the third hour and the driver's refusal to pull over, they seriously began to worry the party would never end. Though some of them had become more mentally and physiologically accustomed to their situation.

"What did that say?" Jill asked Beth.

"It was a map."

"To what?"

"Treasure!"

"Oh my god," Angie said. "We need you acting crazy like we need a hole in our head."

"We need a hole in this boat!" someone shouted, half underwater, probably Reeves, by far the drunkest of them all.

Jill shook her head and rubbed Angie's shoulders, trying to keep her spirits up after the loss of Amy, who had panicked and jumped off into the dark about fifty miles earlier. And, hey, it was *still* her birthday, Jill tried to remind them all, and she wanted people to make the most of it. Hell, parties were supposed to be dangerous. Away from the others, Jill gently assured Angie that people would know they were missing soon enough.

Reeves surged up between them right then, and maybe it was because they'd been driving in the dark for so long and all their pupils were so dilated, but Angie could have sworn his eyes rolled over black when he smiled and slid backwards under the water again to swim.

***

Their circle constricted for a bit, increasing the heat, but Angie shivered when someone spun another bottle. This was because every time one of the dudes tried to get a game of Spin the Bottle going, the driver seemed to sense it and whipped the red, air-horned beast back to full throttle. So their resulting panic meant any game quickly degenerated into Truth or Dare instead, which was sort of a mob-mentality comfort food, and a welcome distraction. But every time one of the females tried to keep that game going, they just ended up trading injuries stories all over again.

This time it was Holly, Gaddy, and Sherry trading scars, and listening to them. Angie realized why fairy tales always started with the same word.

"Once, I sprained both wrists and ruptured a disc in my back by moving boxes of books at work," Holly said. "Ended up having surgery on my spine and spent months of rehab in a pool with weights around my ankles. The retired Olympic psycho in charge of my rehabilitation seemed to develop a crush on me, and I started getting worried that she didn't want to see me get better and kept trying to injure me again. Seriously, who puts weights on someone's legs in a pool? How dangerous is that? That's like putting a goddamn pool on a fire truck!"

The group snickered at that.

"Once, I fell about a hundred feet out of this tree at our family's first house," Gaddy said. "It was this huge weeping willow with a broken branch at the top that laid flat across two splits in the trunk. After a week of intense debate, we named it 'The Bridge,' and we would climb up there and stand and look out at everyone's rooftops. And, of course, it finally collapsed when I was on it, dropping me down through about a hundred limbs like someone had just hit the multi-ball reward on a pinball machine. I ended up tangled and hanging upside down over a thick bottom branch, slowly rocking back and forth, trying to cry with the wind knocked out of me. Then I untangled, dropped to the grass, and saw a layer of skin sheered off my left forearm, wrist, and fingertips. I couldn't touch anything for weeks, it stung so bad. See that right above the elbow? Where I'm the wrong color?"

"Racist!" someone laughed.

"Speaking of pinball machines!" Sherry said, going for the one-up. "Our dad actually got us a pinball machine for Christmas once. It was a weird one, though. You know how pinball machines usually have themes, like movies or musicians? Well, this one's theme seemed to be 'pinball,' as it had pictures of '70s-looking guys playing pinball on it! Therefore, I can only assume that the machines *they* were playing also had little dudes playing pinball on them. Turtles all the way down. But me and my brother loved it, and we must have played with it for a whole six to nine minutes. Once, we tried to take it apart. I was reaching up inside to try to get the metal balls out—I had to, had to get them out—and my brother hit the buttons, and something inside blinked, squawked, gave me 500 points, and quickly sliced the top off one of my knuckles. I still have this white line across the bone to this day…"

"I wanna go home," Beth cried behind them, fingers in her ears. It wasn't just the chatter. The party music the driver had started their trip with was blasting was even louder now. They instinctually circled the wagons again, around another Devil's Cut empty nodding in the water. Jill used the opportunity to spin it once, twice, three times, until it finally slowed to point somewhere near her, and they all got the idea at the same time.

"So, do you wanna play or what?" she asked them, already knowing the answer.

"I think everybody's already kissed everybody," Reeves said, half under water where he lived now.

"Let's do a Ouija board," Angie said, and those who knew her well groaned. She was always keen on this idea, had been all her life really. Besides the fact that Ouija-ing it up was her preferred party game (because it didn't pair everyone off like Spin the Bottle), she also had the sort of love for the game that automatically came from parents throwing the boards in the trash as fast as she could buy them.

Before her mother regretted finally giving in to buy her an "official" one, Angie had played her own version of the "game" with a variety of other objects, some even alive. Like the time she gently laid her fingers on the back of the turtle she'd found on the Morse code white lines of their street, letting it guide them both to the safety of the gutter, asking the question in her head:

"If he steps on that cigarette, I'll die before I'm twenty. If he steps on that candy wrapper, I'll live forever…"

But her favorite early incarnation was modifying a 1975 Milton Bradley board game called The Bermuda Triangle, which handily supplied its own version of a planchette, a blue amoeba-like cloud with a magnet hidden on the bottom. And when you spun the wrong numbers (or the right numbers depending on your reck- lessness) this dark cloud slid over your tiny, metal-capped ships and plucked them from the game board unseen under your hands, vanishing from their shipping fleets forever. Angie lost the spinner eventually, and she and her friends resorted to a more coopera- tive form of game play, all of them with their tiny fingertips just brushing the edges of the thundercloud as it swept the entire game triangle free of ships. Because of this modification, most of their games lasted one round, or approximately fifteen minutes. So, ex- cept for the delicious sense of doom, sort of the opposite of their predicament, at least when it came to duration.

"How the hell would we play that game, stuck in the back of a hot tub, lost on the back roads of Kentucky?" Lund scoffed, always a problem.

"I don't think the driver's lost," Beth hissed.

"What part is the 'Ouija' though?" Jill asked. She seemed game, as usual. "The thing or the board?"

"I think it's the board?" someone muttered.

"Yeah, all the letters," someone agreed.

"So even if you could play it without the thing," Jill said. "You can't play without the board."

"Planchette!" someone shouted, probably Lund.

"Sounds like lunch," Jill laughed.

"It's shaped like a heart."

"With a few more splinters."

"We don't need a board. The board is the water. And the thing…"

"Planchette!"

"…can be a bottle."

They remained skeptical.

"No, no, this can work," Angie said, desperate now. "We can designate one person 'yes' and one person 'no,' but, wait, what do we do about the letters?"

"Easy, there's, what, nine of us left?" Lund said. "That's three letters each, like how you had to text before smart phones! So 'one' is 'A-B-C'…"

"'Two' would be 'A-B-C,' bro," Reeves spit from a wave as the fire truck took another unlit turn. "'One' didn't have any letters on it. I know my phone is old as fuck."

"And four letters were on number 'seven'."

"Fine! Forget it. We'll just do 'yes' or 'no.'"

"You can't play Ouija boards without the board," someone muttered again, but it was too dark to know who, and they did it anyway.

***

Trapped in the tub, they drank, then drank some more. Then they drank like their lives depended on it. When the alcohol was mostly gone, they found themselves drinking whatever had filled the bottles and cans that bobbed past their faces. When they studied their hands, they found that all their soaking had shriveled their fingertips to tire treads, which gripped the slippery bottles wonderfully now, and, in turn, made their bodies even more conducive to systematic inebriation, even if someone of it was imaginary.

They tried using the Devil's Cut as their planchette, and realized it was surprisingly effective. There was less resistance in the water than on a table surrounded by skeptics, and their hands moved it easily three times as fast. In no time they were deciphering messages.

"There Is No Fire," was the first one they translated, which was a head-scratcher. Angie guessed it had something to do with alerting people to a fire truck that refused to stop. But it would have made more sense if the sirens were flashing, or if the message was delivered to anyone except some drunken hostages.

"Most people think Ouija boards are modern-day lie detectors," Beth said. "Though you can beat both of them the exact same way."

"Oh no," Holly laughed. "Watch her butt for bubbles!" and Beth slugged her in the arm.

"Wait, huh?" Dan was baffled and angry. He was a bit of a bully, like a B-side Reeves.

"She's serious," Gaddy said. "Like, say, if you answer the question, 'Have you been to the Moon,' you just answer, 'Yes,' but then finish in your head with 'Moon Township, Pennsylvania'…"

"Where the heck is that?" Lund asked.

"Have we already started?" Dan asked.

"I think she already lost," Reeves said, blowing bubbles like a baby.

"Have you ever been to Mars?" Lund asked.

"Mars, Pennsylvania, yes," she smiled.

"What the heck is going on in Pennsylvania?" Lund laughed.

They all studied his face a moment, then threw up their hands and burst out laughing.

"Whoops, there's another loophole," Angie said. "Be an idiot!"

"All right, since we clearly have all night to burn, did we do this yet?" Jill asked. "I'd like to propose a toast. To myself and another successful journey around the sun!"

"Someone already said that," Lund mumbled, not confident enough to say it was him.

"That is some deep shit," Dan said.

"Huh?"

"I said, that is some deep shit!" Dan yelled.

"Yes, we are in some deep shit!" Lund yelled back.

"I can't take much more of this fucking music!" Reeves said, punching the side of the truck hard enough that they felt it in the water around them.

They went back to their games.

At some point, the bottle spelled out "Yield." Or maybe it was "Wield." But there was enough of a debate for the bullies to start rummaging the back of the truck for weapons again.

***

Messages in bottles and "yes" and "no" questions became the thing for a little while after that argument, which Angie considered a waste of time as Reeves just asked everyone if they wanted to die, then struggled to point the bottle at himself, who had been designated the "Yes" as long as he wasn't trying to swim and bump into everyone's legs. Angie wished they'd hoisted Reeves up on some shoulders to play "Chicken" like they had when the night started. Then someone could flush him over the side instead, to get sucked under those awful wheels in turn, just like Amy, slurped up like a gnat vacuumed in your yawn.

But Reeves just kept getting pats on the back for his jokes, and his vigorous laps, until she saw Jill recoil at something she felt between his shoulder blades.

"What the hell is that!" Jill said, looking at her hand like she'd been bit.

"I don't know. A scab or something. I musta got cut…"

"Do you see that on his back?" Jill said, almost falling over to move away from him. "What's growing on his back?"

Angie was convinced it was a fin, but he'd vanished under the waves again. People started talking about their drinks being spiked and all measure of hallucinations, and Angie was colder than she'd ever been in her life.

"I think we've been poisoned," Beth said. "If not by the beers, then by this water."

Jill snorted at this, and Angie looked her over, noticing her carefully cultivated "Hitchcock" look tonight, the "suicide blonde," head down and eyes perpetually narrowed, like she was always gazing over an invisible newspaper.

"Maybe we're on a prison bus right now, headed for jail for our crimes," Angie said. "And we're not in a pool at all. This is just a bus filled with urine and sweat, and we're all handcuffed to each other and pissing all over the floor…"

"Stop!" Beth said, fingers in her ears again.

"Are our crimes really so bad?" Jill asked them all.

The bottle floated towards where Reeves was kicking in the corner, and Jill, Beth, and Angie recoiled from it as if burned.

Finally they were out of all alcohol for good, no bottles or beer cans to warm their bellies or their brains, and Angie closed her eyes with both hands on the rail, feeling the rumble of the road, understanding that she now knew these invisible wheels even more intimately than her own body.

***

They wouldn't have known it, but it was an uncharacteristically hot night for that time of year anyway. But certainly not too hot for Kentucky, and once they left Bardstown Road, and once she counted the shadows of nineteen overpasses without ever turning, Angie knew the party had to be heading for somewhere even colder for their final destination. True hell on Earth. Indiana.

Few people remembered that the final circle in Dante's *Inferno* was actually ice, but she did. And Indiana was hell all right. Or worse, maybe they were headed for the Tenth Circle, that redneck baby-talk-y hybrid of a name, the DMZ where the worst people she'd ever known lived and breathed (but rarely worked), a limbo they referred to as "Kentuckiana," where she'd been drunkenly assaulted by authority figures at least twice while passing through.

There would be no help there, she decided, and she vowed to end the journey, by any means necessary, before she crossed that line. But she was too tired to plot, and Angie was well on her way to the sweet comfort of hypothermic sleep when she saw Lund using a broken bottle to cut a stretch of fire hose. They'd long since stopped playing their game by then, as too many planchettes floated and clinked in their midst, seemingly desperate for more terrifying questions, but the acceleration of the truck when they played also was a strong deterrent.

Angie watched Lund labor another moment, confused. They'd long since decided climbing off as the driver barreled along at breakneck speed was suicide. Then she finally understood what he was doing.

He wanted to drain the pool.

As she watched, Lund sucked on one end of the hose, and successfully siphoned the green soup from the pool around them to splash out onto the street, but people weren't feeling the plan like he'd hoped. And once the pool water was down to their ankles and their bodies were even more at the mercy of a wind that whisked the moisture from their swim suits and underwear, no one was looking at Lund like a hero. And just that quickly, his party was over.

Chubby Spencer S. Lundergaard, the only reveler wearing glasses, sometimes referred to as *Lord of the Fries* while growing up, became the party's next distraction. And he wasn't even targeted by the regular assailants, Reeves and Dan, but by everyone else instead. It was Beth who punched him in the mouth first, with a fist full of bottle. It shattered and his eye rode the shards over the rail, a comet trail of optic nerve and white lidless surprise. Beth stepped back in surprise, hands out in surrender. More joined the fight, but so far away from civilization, and so far into the depressing blackened, blasted-out strip-mall void that was Kentuckiana, Angie couldn't really see who was who anymore. But she heard three or four wet bodies tackle Lund and drag him toward the taillights over his protests.

She tried to cover her eyes with her hand before the ritual was illuminated in red, but she couldn't help but peek through her wrinkled fingers before it was over, and she saw Lund's glasses divided as neatly as his head as he was hurled off the truck and headfirst, but with one headlight out, straight into a "Yield" sign. And, agreeable to the end, this was exactly what his skull did to comply under its yellow metal blade.

***

It didn't seem possible, but the driver sped up even more, and Angie felt her ears pop from a change in air pressure. Angie could sometimes make out the black of Reeves' eyes and the whites of Jill's teeth, and she guessed she was smiling at the very real possibility of time travel on her unique leap-day birthday, probably the most memorable birthday party of all time. For the rest of them, though, panic was in full swing, which was its own sort of party.

And in the dark, after battling the rumbles of the road for so long, they'd somehow developed a new form of communication, one that lacked language but was no less clear to them all. At first, she'd assumed there were too many bottles for their game, but now she realized they were all still playing. Hugging their own chests, corralling floating cans and bottles between their legs, periodically holding their breath to stop their chattering teeth, and long, slow blinks, occasionally flicking a bottle and mouthing the letters as it pointed at them all in turn, speaking to them more clearly than anyone could have predicted.

Angie read their bodies, all of them roughly translated as, "We're in this together," or maybe "We're fucked," which meant the same thing really.

After a silence that felt like five years and five hundred more miles, Jill whispered that she missed her cat, wondering who would feed him.

"A cat's future is even more limited than our own," Jill went on. "You know why? Because of one simple fact. If you hold them like toddlers with their feet barely touching the ground, a cat can only walk backwards. Did you know that the only instance of this affliction recorded in human beings is in a swimming pool?"

This all sounded reasonable, and even like something Lund would have said, but he was long gone. Angie tried to get a head count, and she thought about how there were more women than men left in the end. She attributed this to the hidden exercises they could always do under the waves, to tread water forever, those muscles they develop in secret when they were digging half-moons into their palms with their own fingernails under the covers while their fathers over-explain things, all the while smiling, smiling, smiling through their eyeteeth.

Jill grabbed Angie's face, and she tried real hard to keep listening, but she was captivated by a sleek, slack-jawed visage, somewhat resembling Dan's grinning, catatonic face, sinking beneath the suds, dragged down to be consumed by an unseen force, never to resurface.

"You see, in a pool it's almost impossible to walk forward when your body divides the surface of the water between the tips of your toes and your nostrils," Jill explained like this was the answer to everything. "You have no choice but to never go forward. You will back up forever."

Angie believed her, ever before her embrace, even before their kiss, and together they discovered the last two warm places in the world.

***

They flew past something huge, some sort of gargantuan illumination on the horizon. And it was moving. Then they saw the rectangle flickering like a massive television through the trees, and they understood it was the drive-in movie again, and they could just make out the end credits scrolling up the screen.

Some of them stopped shivering in the wind, focusing through their shock and haze, and some finally realized that only an hour and a half could have passed if the movie was just ending, a maximum of three hours if it was a typical double-feature, the requisite running time of a motion picture and exactly the amount of time they had paid the driver for.

Then they forgot all this math just as quickly, as if their thoughts drained out their ears and onto the asphalt as freely as the last of their fetid pool water.

Someone sprung up like a porpoise, saluted anyone who remained, and then someone jumped off into the night. It was so dark, and it happened so fast, there was no time for her to ascertain the identity, even illuminated by the occasional lightning flash that she swore originated eleven hundred miles away in Bermuda. But if Angie had to hazard a guess, she would have said it was Reeves. Even after all the death at his hands, she was sorry to see him go. The pool would miss his body heat and manic exercises dearly.

At some point, Beth cracked and never came back, screaming until she was hoarse. And when she hit top volume and some of the bottles shattered in the puddles at their feet, they were suddenly driving past a real-live school bus full of kids' butts and faces on their way home from some other game, a pink-and-yellow flash of skin heading in the opposite direction, like a snapshot from the yearbook of their former lives, and those kids just screamed back at Beth, thinking it was a party, which it was, of course.

It was the last party, where every party in the world had the potential to end up if it tried hard enough.

***

They all held hands in the glow of the taillights, a red haze that signaled death for most of the ride, but now marked a doorway to possible escape. Their eyes watered, but their blinking was stolid.

They all jumped together.

And they landed not on the road, but on the grass, intact, alive.

The truck had stopped.

For how long, no one knew, with their bodies so numb from the wind and the drink and the time that had long ago been rendered meaningless.

They were deep in the woods, but still in someone's yard.

At a party.

Colorful streamers and balloons were tangled in the trees, huge "Happy Birthdays!" scrawled in childlike letters and glimmering in the flickering light of a tall bonfire, and the remaining partiers silently circled it to get warm. Or maybe they were circling Jill. Angie couldn't be sure. Further off on the horizon were some power lines, and a bundle of transformers, possibly a tall fence surrounded by barbed wire. It was tough to see in the dark and her bloodshot eyes had yet to adjust to a world not made of taillights.

The cab door opened, and the driver stepped out. He was a huge man, wearing headphones, unplugged and dangling, and a black eyepatch hovered indecisive between his eyebrows. The bundle of dollars they'd paid him at the beginning of the night fluttered from the chest pocket of his overalls, ends flapping in the wind like a rattlesnake. Then the money flew free from his pocket, one dollar after the other, leaving a wake of cash behind him, and he made no attempt to retrieve it. On the dashboard, a crackling TV monitor was visible, with the now-empty party pool flickering on the screen.

The driver frowned and looked over the group, mouth working as he scanned their bodies, naked and streaked with blood, piss, and beer. Sexless and indistinguishable.

"Goddamn, you kids sure know how to celebrate," the driver said, sliding the eyepatch over his left eye, then his right. He laughed. "Though some people would argue a surprise party is a form of aggression."

Though no one could see it happen, they all imperceptively turned to each other, fingertips gently caressing the rough, heart-shaped edges of their worst ideas, and though no one could hear it, a message was both sent, and received.

And everyone who was left fell upon the driver, ripping and

piercing, sometimes with broken bottle shards for teeth, tearing him down to the ground, down to their level of understanding to render him recognizable as the perfect asset for any party:

Ribbons.

Once transformed into warm pile of red, streaming party favors, they placed his body on top of the long metal coffin behind the cab, and one of them came from the bonfire with a flaming branch, green end popping and cracking as it blackened.

The fire truck burned like it was born to. But there were other trucks at the party, too. New trucks with gleaming chrome and no rust, not burdened by the embarrassment of a conversion to a bullshit party pool or undergrad dance wagon, and well-muscled men sat in the trailers, coils of hose between their legs, drinking beer and eating popcorn, but making no effort to stop the blaze. Eventually, more vehicles arrived, and faceless men in jumpsuits and fogged-up visors began to douse the flames, the torrents from their hoses filling their pool back up to the brim. Naked and against all instincts, Angie ran through the roar and glare of the sirens to climb aboard the nearest fire truck she could find. And on this truck, black now instead of red, she sat in a seat facing the wrong way, next to more astronauts and anonymous shades, and she squeezed her hands locked behind her back, smoothing valleys back in her fingerprints, dreaming of rolling through bright-lit streets and crowds very soon, speaking silently with those fingers, her breath and the tip of her nose drawing hearts on her window, dreaming of more celebrations, in places teeming with secret highway rites, the wind blowing the blood from her dirty blond hair before it could dry as she breathed in a world she was no longer convinced existed.

Behind her, within the black husk of the smoldering party bus, she saw Reeves reemerge from the trees, slick and gray, striding through the billows of smoke and the bonfire now turned wildfire, to climb back onto their engine. Indifferent to the pyre, he stepped up the chrome stairs, back up into the boiling cauldron, now overflowing with water and flame. She watched the fin on his back and his perfect body cut through the waves like he was claiming the deep end of any pool, and Angie leaned out into the wind as far as she could without falling, still able to sense him through the growing distance and fading distortion and shimmer of heat. She could still feel his cold skin pressed against her own, warming her, then cooling them both, then perfectly acclimating to the world until they were invisible.

PINS

S.P. MISKOWSKI

"**Y**ou've got to hold the pins in both your hands," the psychic explained. Her voice was gritty and low. The last word was almost a growl. "Cover one hand with the other, like this, and wait."

"For how long?" Helen asked.

"Just wait," the psychic told her. The woman must have smoked a pack of cigarettes a day, judging by the depth of that voice. She continued to stare across the table at Helen, who was starting to wonder if the woman's lopsided grin was a sign of backwardness.

All of this—stopping for an afternoon meal of biscuits at the diner; getting the Grand Prix tuned up by the only mechanic for miles around; wandering into the psychic's dusty yard, after reading the faded lettering on the gate—the entire layover in this town the size of a trailer park had been the twins' idea.

Julie and Debbie threw a tantrum, insisting they would *die* if they couldn't stretch their legs. Twelve hours on the road without stopping and even Helen felt the need for solid ground beneath her feet. Against her better judgment she had pulled over, and the rest of the day had taken a turn.

***

The diner was operated by a gal named Barb, a World War II widow with a patriotic streak who covered every inch of wall space with various sizes of flags and framed photos of soldiers. Every photograph bore a date written in black ink in the lower right-hand corner. Helen was afraid to ask if the date indicated when the picture was taken or when the soldier had died.

"Do they all live in this town?" Debbie asked, pointing at the walls.

"Used to, at one time or another," said Barb. She set the glass bottle of molasses syrup next to the butter dish. "Most were stationed over at the base, a couple of miles away."

"We saw the freeway sign," said Julie. "Y'all are sure out of the way, Mama said."

Helen smiled at Barb and shook her head, dismissing her daughter's idle talk. She didn't want extra attention from the locals. This was exactly why she tried to avoid these hokey little places. In this part of the state most towns were a few roadside shacks and a trailer park sharing a zip code. Lately she stuck to the more populated areas, where a woman with twins in a Grand Prix wouldn't be the most interesting thing to appear all week.

"Motor-mouth," Helen said to her daughter as soon as Barb walked away.

Julie pulled a hurt face. Then she stuck out her tongue and Helen put a hand on her wrist to let her know the routine wasn't funny any more.

"Ow," Julie whined. "Hurts."

"Little girl," said Helen. "Stop it right now. I mean it."

Julie quit whining and sat up straight. She picked at the biscuits on her plate with a fork.

Debbie studied the photos on the wall next to their booth. "Mama," she said. "Are these men all gone? Did they die in a war?"

Helen ignored the question. She felt uneasy with all the dead men in uniform staring out at her. "There," she said when she spied a business flyer taped next to the cash register. From her purse she retrieved pencil stubs and two pages of a small notebook. "Whichever one writes down all that information first gets a dime for the gumball machine."

***

Debbie sat silently beside Julie in the backseat, on the short drive to the mechanic's garage. She held a grape jawbreaker lodged securely inside her right cheek to keep her sister tantalizingly aware it was just out of reach.

"Stay here until I come back," Helen told the girls. She kept her eyes on them all the way to the office, a metal desk surrounded by smudged windows occupying one corner of the building. The rubber and oil smell reminded her of her father, a man who had never seen a carburetor he couldn't rebuild; nothing like her husband, Roy. Her husband had been a fastidious man. Roy would have cut off his arm before he'd touch the dirty engine of a car. For the Grand Prix there had been a shop in Decatur with a 'specialist.' Roy wouldn't trust anyone else.

Helen felt a rush handing over the keys to this stranger with his initials—J.B.—stitched on the pocket of his coveralls. She said yes to an oil change and a tune-up. J.B. offered to throw in tire rotation because he wasn't busy. But she told him she didn't need it right now. He recommended the family visit the military museum across the road, if the girls wanted to kill time.

When Helen fetched the twins from the backseat Debbie's ponytail was askew and Julie sported a bright red circle next to one eye. The jawbreaker was still lodged in Debbie's right cheek where it skidded and clacked against her teeth.

The museum was a long rectangle made of sandstone fronted by a nearly empty parking lot. They were making a beeline for the lobby when Julie spotted the ornate, weather-beaten letters on a gate to their left. "What's a p-p-sick-ick?" she asked.

"It says fizz-ick," Debbie chided.

Helen had a moment of self-loathing over the way she'd ne-
glected the girls' education on the road. She couldn't keep this trip
going forever.

"Psychic," she said. "It means a fortune teller."

"Oh," said Debbie, waving one hand nonchalantly. "Of course.
Sigh-kick. You ought to get your fortune told, Mama."

"I don't believe in it," she lied. A placard on the museum door
urged visitors to honor the dead by offering a donation of five dollars. Compared to the museum, the psychic's posted rates seemed
like a bargain.

***

"How long does it take?" Helen asked the psychic. Two dollars
and twenty minutes later she was cupping a batch of straight pins
in her right hand and holding her left hand over them like a lid,
waiting.

The twins occupied a world of their own playing with three
kittens on the floor on overlapping rugs. The kittens dashed and
pounced and rolled, crashing into one another to the twins' de-
light.

The psychic opened a window at her elbow and lit a cigarette.
Just as Helen suspected, the woman inhaled with the obvious pleasure of a chain-smoker. She wasn't sure what they were waiting
for but she longed for a puff of the woman's cigarette. She was
about to ask again how long she had to hold the pins, when she
became aware of a burning sensation in her right palm. The metal
pins heated faster and faster in her cupped hand until she flinched
and let out a yelp. The pins, ten straight and three bent, scattered
across the table.

The psychic perked up and seemed interested, at last. She
stubbed out her cigarette in a plastic ashtray shaped like a cat,
and moved closer. Hunched over the tabletop she made a series of
grunting noises while she examined where and in which patterns

and directions the pins had fallen.

Helen studied the spot in the center of her hands where she had felt her flesh burning. She couldn't see a singe or a scratch any-where—proof of a trick, was her guess. The psychic had to show off a little, to make it worth two dollars.

"Do you look at cards, too?" Helen asked.

"Huh?"

"I thought you would read cards."

"No cards," the psychic mumbled. "I read the pins. They tell everything."

"Well, if you say so."

"These double sets of lines here," the psychic said, pointing.

"Yes." Helen nodded. Four of the pins had landed together and lay parallel and close to one another.

"Have you got another set of twins at home?"

Helen was stunned at the reminder of her home outside Atlanta, more than a thousand miles away. She was equally stunned by the swift, sharp memory of what she'd left in the master bedroom, covered in a chenille bedspread. She shook her head because words wouldn't come to mind quickly enough. Suddenly she was afraid every detail was somehow visible to this stranger living on the fringe of an almost empty town in a state Helen had never ex-pected to visit.

"No," she said. "I've just got the two daughters."

The psychic seemed unconvinced. "Then you've had another set and lost it?"

The words the woman used didn't make sense to her. It? Lost? They weren't talking about misplaced keys.

"Sorry," said the psychic, with a glance at the preoccupied twins. "Have you lost a pregnancy?"

This had to be a standard question asked by charlatans, an edu-cated guess based on how a customer held her head, how tired she seemed, and what kind of outfit she was wearing. For the past five weeks Helen had tended toward Capri pants and a simple navy cotton blouse. As the trip grew longer she had stopped applying eye shadow and mascara each morning, settling on lipstick and a dusting of powder across her nose. Maybe she was falling short in her grooming habits. The psychic must have a list of questions to try out, and she had chosen this one based on some telltale sign, something off about Helen's manner, or sad and sloppy about the girls' appearance.

"No," Helen said. "No, I never…"

The woman lifted her face to look into Helen's eyes. Whatever she found there, she ducked her head again at once and returned to her contemplation of the pins.

"These four lines, see how perfect they are? How they line up? You hardly ever see this."

"What else could they mean?" Helen asked. In a far corner of the room the twins were trying quietly and gently to corral the kittens.

"The rest of this pattern is confused, so many directions at once. I'm not sure…"

"It's all right," Helen told her.

"No," the woman told her. "No, this is very unusual."

"That's all right, you gave me a lot to think about, and I've enjoyed it," Helen said. "Girls!" She motioned for the twins to follow her out of the trailer.

"Here," said the psychic. She picked up the payment jar, selected the two bills Helen had paid, and pressed them into her hand. "I couldn't help you."

"I don't expect a refund."

"No," the psychic insisted, backing away, putting her hands behind her back. "I couldn't help you."

***

The Grand Prix was ready when they crossed the road and greeted J.B. at the garage. The total was far less than Helen expected. She

checked the itemized list and paid. She wasn't in a position to argue with a good deal.

Once they were settled in with snacks and sodas they were ready
to get back on the road. Helen adjusted the rearview mirror. Julie
and Debbie had the half-sleepy, half-sulking expression they affected when they weren't having fun but couldn't find a good reason to complain. The jawbreaker was long gone. The girls shared
a bag of potato chips.

Both twins studied their mother's face in the reflection of the
rearview mirror. They had stopped asking when their dad would
catch up to them on vacation, and then stopped mentioning Roy
at all. The miles were wearing all of them down.

Helen drove out of the garage parking lot. The ground level
night-lights were coming on at the museum and the white stone-
work posed a mute white shadow behind them. In less than a mile
the sparse lighting of the so-called town would be absorbed in the
dark, vast desert. Boulders would rise on either side of the car and
their silhouettes would climb into the black sky. But for the first
half an hour Helen exulted in the speed of the car and the emptiness of the landscape on all sides. She could never have talked Roy
into a meandering road trip, and wasn't that the whole point? They
were free of everything Roy wanted.

Helen blushed. She was quick to backtrack, to find reasons
much more noble than the only one she had needed. The idea of
self-justification made her jumpy.

When the twins fell asleep she would break loose. Without the
constraint of their fear she could drive eighty miles an hour and
imagine driving a hundred. At eighty she could feel a veil or skin
splitting and tearing away, opening swiftly and vanishing into the air.

She knew the rigid smile of her husband would be collapsing by
now, resting soft and sticky against his jaw. He was a handsome
man only recently going to seed, ignoring an extra twelve pounds,
saying yes to another cocktail, letting less and less pretty waitresses
make a fuss over his needs, and ordering dessert with every meal.

In truth Helen was only surprised it hadn't happened sooner, when she was younger, when she loved him and wanted to lash out at every lazy, arrogant girl who stared right through her at Roy. The hotel porter who only spoke to Roy, the car salesman who told a joke about a big-breasted wife while Helen was in the room, when she was the one making the down payment. Every slight she had endured and every time Roy had bruised her face and arms so she couldn't go out for days.

When it finally happened she was surprised by the swiftness and simplicity of the moment. She had often thought, if it came to that, if it came to what she always expected between herself and Roy, she would put the twins to sleep first, mix a sedative into their bedtime glass of milk, turn their faces to the wall. This was a vague assumption. She had never planned it through step by step, never anticipated the means or the opportunity but she recognized both when they appeared.

How could a psychic see what she herself had never known with certainty until it occurred? The woman was just an entertainer making things up for bored local housewives, and truckers.

Miles of burnt brush decorated both sides of the road. Charred plumes, blackened weeds; the upswept remains of some native plant Helen didn't recognize ran parallel to the painted white lines. She had an unexpected memory from childhood, the night her mother set fire to the Christmas tree. Not only the lights and the tree itself but all of the presents burned to nothing. A corner of the living room had been reduced to a blackened hole. Her mother was cheerful for the first time in years while she recounted the story to a friend and explained how her family had learned from their loss. She never said what they had learned.

Bile rose in Helen's throat until she could taste it. She swallowed it back, forced it down as she had been doing for days. A dose of Pepto Bismol would help at the next stop. She couldn't risk seeing a doctor, no matter how far from home. She could lie about her name but her age was all too apparent these days and she could do nothing to disguise the car or the girls.

For years she had dreamed of running away, leaving her life and herself behind. Now she knew it didn't work that way. No matter where they were headed, she was stuck with all of this, as much as she had been stuck with Roy.

The twins were fast asleep. She popped open the car ashtray, fished a stolen cigarette from her purse, and lit it. With the window down and the speedometer climbing, she could almost pretend she was on her own, with all the time in the world.

DEEP INTO THE SKIN

MATTHEW M. BARTLETT

The town of Hulse sits on a gnarled peninsula that juts from the face of Massachusetts like the chin of a Halloween witch. And me, I'm a Hulse beach rat, born and raised. I spent twenty-seven years breathing in the town's ocean air, absorbing its sand into the heels of my feet. Its name is inked into the skin over my heart. I never in a million years thought I'd leave. But I did, in the winter of 2007. I gathered whatever I could fit in my car and fled across the state to Springfield, and brother, I'm never going back.

I ran my own shop back then. Mikey's Ink Chamber was the name, but I just called it the Chamber. We were at the far end of an unnamed strip mall on a long, desolate stretch of road between commercial districts. Most of the storefronts had long since been vacated; besides the Chamber, all that remained was a quiet electronics repair shop and The Wash Spot, a laundromat whose interior consisted largely of orange Out-of-Order signs.

It started on a February night, just before closing time. I was coming out of the scrub room when Susan, my cashier and bookkeeper, pushed her head through the black velvet curtains between my workstation and the sales floor. "The deposit slips are done and I've swept up," her disembodied head said. Then she stepped through the curtain, became a whole person again. "Do you want me to stay until you're done?"

"No need," I said. "I won't be long."

"Then…can you walk me to my car?"

Now, Susan may be small and slender, but she's a scrapper. A few years back a tough-looking girl had burst into the shop yelling something about getting one's own boyfriend and leaving other girls' boyfriends be. "Outside," Susan had said, and right there in the parking lot she climbed all over the girl like a spider with fists. Before the other girl knew it she was sitting on the curb with a black eye and a loose tooth, spitting blood into the snow.

So any other time this would have been an unusual request. But three nights earlier, Seasick Pete, my old mentor and the proprietor of Skull Kiss Body Art in nearby Deepwater, had been found murdered in his shop, sprawled and bloodied and broken in his chair. His T-shirt had been pulled up over his enormous belly, strange symbols carved deep into the skin around his navel. The killer had dragged Pete's machine all over his face and left it jammed into his mouth. They hadn't emptied the cash register. Instead they used it to stave in the side of poor Pete's head.

A local cop came by the night after the murder to question me. Did I know anyone mad at old Pete, someone maybe got a botch job, a misspelling, infection, whatever. I had no idea, I'd said. Pete had drifted out of my life some time back. Not that there was any animosity—he and I were just different. He was a mile a minute talker, one of those guys who tells you everything about himself within ten minutes of having met you. But he was a good guy, and had a good rep as an artist and a professional. When the cop was through with his questions, he gave me all the grisly details. It was like he was savoring them.

"It's one dead guy, Susan," I said. "I doubt someone's targeting medium-talent ink slingers. Maybe he got tangled up in dope, or townie bullshit. Think about the kind of customers he took on. Nothing to worry about."

"Mikey," she said, raising her painted-on eyebrows. "Would. You please. Walk me. To my car?"

I went to the back and grabbed my coat. We hurried across the lot through the frostbite cold, the wind lashing at our skin, stinging our eyes. The moon hung high up in the cloudless sky, thinner than an albino's eyebrow hair. The only significant source of light was the pollen-coated streetlight over Susan's rusted-out Corolla, flickering a bleary yellow, making the parking lot look like some old German movie. The other shops had closed. The road sat quiet, devoid of travelers, tourists long gone.

"Maybe they'll head over to BodyPunk and kill Dominant Gene," Susan said as she slid into the front seat and started the engine. "You never liked him."

She took off, engine revving. I jogged back across the lot and into the shop. I was in the back wiping down my workstation when I heard the bell jingle, which meant that Susan forgot her purse, as she always does. I went into the shop to give her shit about it, and stopped cold.

Standing at the glass counter was a strange little assemblage of people, the most striking of the three a tall, curvilinear woman in a blinding white dress, with red hair right out of a shampoo commercial. Next to her stood a squat, roundish man jammed into a black suit. He was bald but for a ring of longish white hair circling his head, tangled brown eyebrows like a toddler's scribbles. His papercut of a mouth was curled into a tiny frown. In front of the two stooped a dazed-looking girl who couldn't have been much older than eighteen. She was short, shock-blonde, clad in shredded jeans and a faded black T-shirt whose iron-on logo had long since flaked away, leaving an abstract impressionist painting of reds and yellows and blues.

"We're closed," I said, and the man walked over to the door and locked it.

Oh God, I thought, *they are going to kill me.*

***

From my sophomore year up until the time I left Hulse, I was the kid who'd decided to never remove his Halloween costume. I hid my face under a fearsome beard. My closet was black as coal. I was all boots and buckles, tattoos and piercings: canine bites and the Earl, and three others known only to me and to the middle-aged masseuses who populate the neon-lit parlors that line Hog Island Boulevard. I'm six-foot, fuck-you inches, too, but I can't help that. I also can't do anything about the scar that runs from the side of my nose up to my temple.

You want a laugh? Have a look at my freshman yearbook picture. The requisite plaid shirt, buttoned at the collar. A helmet of wavy brown hair, buck teeth framed in a counterfeit grin. A weak chin that melted into a neck better suited to a swan. I was a mama's boy by default, as Pop had decamped for sunnier, childless climes before I was old enough to know his name. A mama's boy without a mama, in fact, because she was taken from me a year before that picture was taken, stolen away by a relentless cancer that spread through her midsection like a spray of buckshot.

I was every name the rough kids hurled at me and more. A nerd, a spaz, a book jockey. My unofficial first tattoos were bruises the size of fists. So I buried that lost, anxious kid under layers of leather. I inked him up and I covered his face. But he was still here under all that costumery. Shy, diffident. Repelled by confrontation. A coward in the costume of a badass.

The scar? I didn't win it in some bar fight or arcade brawl. I was eight. I'd been riding bikes with the neighborhood kids, when Frankie Moore turned onto Stafford Road and came after me. I sped out onto Nantasket Avenue, right into the path of an old Cadillac. Guy in the car hit his brakes just as I hit mine. I somersaulted over the handlebars and slid on my face for a few yards, ending up in a heap at the curb. The driver screamed at me as Frankie beat it. For eight weeks my face was a horror show. What remains, mostly under the beard, is a patch of mottled, gravel-pocked skin. And the scar.

***

The man cleared his throat theatrically, and then spoke. His voice was the croak of a frog—a chain-smoking frog. "I understand that it's after hours," he said, "but I have a job for you, and it needs to be done tonight. Consider your life to be the compensation."

"I just have to get set up," I said, and the girl bolted. She hit the door, fumbled with the latch, and stumbled off into the night.

"Be right back," said the man, and he walked calmly through the door after her.

I have principles. I do. I know right from wrong, and good from bad, and I knew the minute I saw the dazed—let's face it, drugged—look in the eyes of that girl that this whole situation was very wrong, and very, very bad. And the moment she fled, I knew, at least as far as the fundamentals, why Seasick Pete lost his life. He, too, had principles. And he'd made the fatal mistake of fighting for them.

The woman shrugged and came around the counter, hips swiveling. She walked right into my personal space. "You're tall," she said. Her swollen lips shone a startling red. She smelled like strawberries and cigarettes. She leaned in, her breast pushing up against my upper arm, the tip of her nose touching my neck, those terrifying lips closing in. "And you smell good."

"It's just soap," I said, and the door slammed open. The man and the girl came in, his hand gripping the back of her neck. The girl was smiling now, her lips pulled up over her teeth in a pained smile. Her pupil were pinpricks, her terror tucked somewhere back behind them.

"Well, I see we're getting cozy," the man said. "That's good. Why don't you be a good host and show us in?"

I led the trio back into the work area. As I prepped the table, the woman pulled the girl's T-shirt over her head and dropped it on the floor, yanked at her jeans so that the waist rested just above her pubic bone. She might as well have been tearing the clothing from a doll. Then she grabbed the girl's hair and led her over to the chair as the man pulled from inside his coat a snapshot. He handed it to me.

It was a picture of an antique, dusk-blue Ouija-type board laying on an Oriental carpet. Across the top it read SÉANCE BOARD in a lightning bolt font. Below that sat the letters of the alphabet in two frowning rows, then the digits one through zero in a straight line. One on side the word YES sat in the grinning mouth of a pointy-horned goat. On the other side the word NO in the frowning maw of a curly-horned ram. Below it all the word GOODBYE, written like dripping blood.

"The whole thing?" I said, failing to keep my voice from trembling. "The full length of her torso?"

"Yes." He ran a finger along her left side. She flinched. "The top here," he said. "That's important."

The girl began to weep. The man and the woman stared at me, hard-faced.

People come in drunk to get tattoos, I thought, *and I do it without a blink. They come in high, go under the needle at the urging of snickering friends. I don't turn them away. I can do this. Get through it. If I try to stop it, if I refuse, I'll be as dead as Seasick Pete, and it could go worse for her, prolong this nightmare. After, I'll call the police. I'll get the license number and report it. The minute they're gone. The minute I'm safe.*

Resolved, then. I started the prep, telling myself this was just another job, a willing client. I made direct eye contact and I explained the process as I went. I used the tender, neutral tone I use for first -timers. After a short time, her tears ran dry. She just stared at me with those big eyes, like she was concentrating. I soaped up a towel and gently ran it over the contours of her body. Her nostrils flexed slightly when I uncapped the rubbing alcohol and wiped her chest and stomach.

"Relax," I told her. "Breathe. In your nose. Out your mouth."

She did as she was told. Her breath was grape-flavored gum and animal fear.

"Have you eaten?"

She nodded.

"Then here we go."

I started up the machine. At the buzzing sound, she closed her eyes tightly. When the needle first touched her trembling flesh, she hissed. Tears welled anew in her eyes. I looked over at the couple and jerked my head toward the box of tissues on the counter. "Would you mind wiping her eyes?"

It was hard to keep the anger from my voice, the disgust. The woman looked at me fiercely and with defiance, but she did it.

For the next several hours, the only noise was that of the needle doing its work. I surprised myself by falling into my usual sort of trance state, as I would under normal circumstances—the room softened and shimmered, the walls retreating until they were a faraway blur, taking the grim watching pair with them. There was only me and the canvas of skin, and the work. I added my own small flourishes to the symbols on the séance board, elongating the letters, adding flames and fangs to the eyes of the goat and the ram. I felt no fear, only a hazy, prolonged ecstasy. It may have been the last peaceful moment of my life.

A few hours later, I blinked, and the room was back in focus. The job was complete. I felt hung over and drained. I applied the bandages and recited the boilerplate instructions for cleaning and caring for the new tattoo, handed the man an aftercare guide. Fear rushed back into my system, bringing with it a discomfiting pairing of nausea and powerful hunger. *Now they'll kill me,* I thought. But they didn't. The girl stood, shivering despite the heat, and slowly dressed herself. The three walked out into the showroom and I followed.

"Now," the woman said to the man. "It has to be done now."

I braced myself as the man walked along the glass counter,

looking at the stuff for sale in the cases: skull rings, dog collars, temporary tattoos, knives, pipes and hookahs. He stopped, placed his fingertip on the glass just over a Scorpion Hand-Guard serrated-edge bowie knife. "That."

I opened the case-back and removed the knife with a trembling hand. I handed it to him. I considered begging for my life as he opened up the knife, examined the blade. Then he nodded at the redhead, who grabbed the girl by her neck and the back of her pants, lifted her, and slammed her face down on the counter so hard that the glass cracked. The man jumped up, one knee on the counter, the other pressed against her shoulder blade, straddling her neck. The woman hopped up and sat on the girl's calves. I backed up until my ass hit the far wall. I didn't avert my eyes. I wish I had.

With his left hand the man grabbed her arm and stretched it out over her head, with his right he began to saw through the flesh of her wrist. The girl screamed. Blood spurted and flowed, dripping down through the crack, into the case, cascading over the countertop on both sides and onto tiled floor. Then he pressed down hard with the blade, veins standing out in his neck, until the bones broke, and then he sawed the rest of the way through. Curled upon the glass like a frightened bug, the hand looked terribly small. The man snatched it up and slid it into the inside pocket of his jacket as though it was a billfold. Then the couple climbed down. The man pulled a cloth from his pocket and tied it around the girl's bleeding stub. Then threw her over his shoulder and without a word the three left. The bell echoed and faded. The silence was awful. I slumped to the ground. I sat there for about a half hour in a haze. Finally, I got up, put on some music, and set about cleaning up the place.

The next morning the bell woke me up. I was curled up on one of the couches in the loft where we display corsets and boots, T-shirts and bondage gear. I remembered standing there in tears the night before, the phone in my hand, physically unable to dial. I remember sobbing, gagging, vowing to kill myself. I must have collapsed from exhaustion. I heard the clomp-clomp-clomp of Susan's Doc Martens on the stairs, and I pushed myself up to a seated position. She screamed when she saw me, went up a foot into the air. I was terrified for a second that she'd fall backwards down the stairs. "Holy mother of God," she said, fluttering her hand over her heart. "You scared the shit out of me."

She stopped, sniffed the air like a cat. "I don't think this place has ever been cleaner," she said. "What got into you?"

I swung my legs over the side of the couch and held out my hand. She walked over, fishing a cigarette from her purse as she did so. She slid it between my fingers and sat down next to me. I lit the smoke with shaking hands, and shuddered.

"Do you want to talk about it?" she said.

"You know…I don't think I do," I said. "I'm going home."

She said, "Hey, did you know the counter's cracked?"

***

Hulse is a town on the decline. It's plagued by the perpetual reek of low tide, its downtown tainted by a heritage of corruption as old as the town itself. The old-style political corruption, of course, graft, bid-rigging, nepotism. But a darker kind of corruption, too. Witch-cults and covens, summoning of the drowned, moon-worship. Longtime residents know by instinct to avoid the sagging shacks along the shoreline. They know to avert their eyes from the dim-lit windows of the houses hugging the cliff-face up to the triumvirate of giant wind turbines that spin in slow motion like the arms of alien clocks.

It had once been a lively and garish place that housed an amusement park, two arcades, countless shops and restaurants and nightclubs. In the mid-nineties the federal government raided the park and shut it down, and the town's reputation of corruption and dark doings, long known locally, hit the front pages of the national papers. Now there are more shuttered shops than open ones. The less well-to-do tourists still file in in the summertime, lounge on the beach in sagging canvas chairs, pick up six-packs at Chuck Tuna's. They ride the restored carousel, the one remaining trace of that old amusement park. They drop their hard-earned savings at the ice cream shop and the crab shack. They sit on the benches with their steaming cups of Dunkin' and watch the seagulls dive and squeal.

It's the townies who stay, who pay for the sins of the disgraced and dead. I counted myself among them, though I managed to hold on to the vain idea that I would remain untouched by the darkness of the town. I kept to the good streets, steered clear of the fire-lit beach parties, and even routinely turned away the stoic, intense men who brought in crude illustrations of ideograms they wanted tattooed on their faces and bodies, arcane, rune-like symbols that filled me with an atavistic revulsion.

In fact, I sent them Seasick Pete's way, telling them he was a better free-hand artist than I, and guaranteeing they'd be happy with his work. It wasn't technically a lie. Pete dealt solely in blackwork, was known for his painstaking detail, thin lines, shading and stippling, deceptively intricate. It was said he worked like the devil was guiding his hand.

Everything I did to avoid the darkness was for nothing. I knew it after the events of that winter night, knew that I'd stayed too long. I was lashed to the town, sewn into its fabric like a long black thread.

So when the invitation arrived, I was not at all surprised. It was sitting in my mailbox among the red-lettered missives from angry creditors, scrawled in purple pen on an otherwise blank white card. *Dear Michael,* (it read), *You comported yourself remarkably well during our recent visit. I want you to know that I exhausted all other ways before resorting to the vulgar display to which I forced you to bear witness, and to take part in.*

This, as ugly as it was, is a last resort, my last attempt at my own version of a ritual that has failed again and again. Cruelty is an essential component of this hopefully final iteration. It is my wish that you join us for the finale. I feel as though all the parties present for the first part of the ritual must be present for the second part—the important part—to work.

I'm sending this invitation with the hope that you understand that your presence is non-negotiable. I'd like to spare us both the effort and unpleasantness associated with bringing you here by force or by coercion. There has been enough unpleasantness.

The invitation concluded with an address, and a date and time. I stared at it for a long while.

***

The tenement stood out stark against a sky bruised and charred like a body someone didn't want identified. Shadows cavorted in the few lit windows, as though people were capering to the same arrhythmic music. A line of red lights above the double-door entrance shone upward, illuminating a trio of bas reliefs depicting medieval figures with their arms raised to the sky. Some dug into their ears with strange, tapered tools. Others clasped both hands over their mouths. I walked through the open wrought iron gate and approached the double doors. I tried the handle, fully expecting it to be locked, but it gave instantly, with a shriek of rust tearing away as the door, loose on its hinge, swung away from me and slammed against the wall.

Windowed doors stood at either end of the grey checkered lobby. I chose the one on the right and made my way up the cement stairs under dim fluorescent lighting. When I reached the door emblazoned with a black, peeling paint 9, I exited the stairwell into a well-lit, red carpeted hallway lined with doors. I continued along until I reached Apartment 9998. The door was metal, painted red, though the paint was peeled away in large swaths, like peeling skin after a sunburn. A fogged-over peephole stared at me like a cataract-clouded eye. A splotch of pink chewing gum faded to the color of flesh stuck like a barnacle by the knob. I knocked, and the door opened.

It was as though I'd walked into some other world. High ceilings, chandeliers like octopi gripping flickering candles in their many tentacles. The walls were hidden behind vast tapestries depicting old woodcuts: blank-faced men swinging truncheons at a tusk-fanged wolf, a woman crouched like a gargoyle on a church rafter as gape-mouthed parishioners stared and pointed from the V-shaped rows of pews below, winged infants with rat kings clutched by the tails in their fat little fists. The room was unfurnished save a long wooden table on which pyramids of incense sent tendrils of smoke up to the Romanesque tin ceiling.

Behind the table stood the trio from the shop. They wore red tunics. The man was noticeably thinner. One of his eyelids was swollen and discolored. Black bruises stained his cheeks and his breath came in terrible howls. The woman looked much the same as she had in the shop, but she seemed to glow with anticipation. She grinned at me. "Watch," she said.

The one-handed girl dropped her tunic. She lifted her breasts and looked at me with fury in her eyes. I avoided her stare and let my eyes fall down to the tattoo. In the candlelit room it seemed to vibrate, the letters shimmying, the goat and the ram mouthing psalms silent but surely blasphemous. I was stunned by the pride I felt—this was surely my finest ink work, a faithful reproduction of the intent of the original, but the small flourishes made it my own.

Then the curved point of a blade appeared from the hollow of the girl's throat. Her eyes widened, then the life drained from them as the blade slid back in like a snake retreating into its black tunnel, and blood spurted out in great arcs. The girl crumpled to the floor.

The man dropped the knife to the floor. It was in reach. I looked down at it.

"Now," the man said, pointing at the woman. His voice was barely audible. "It has to be now. Quickly."

He grabbed the girl under the armpits, his face crumpling with the strain. The woman grabbed her feet. They lifted her onto the altar. From the folds of his robe the man pulled the girl's severed hand. It was purple, stiff with rigor. Someone had inexpertly sewn the tip of the thumb to that of the index finger. The stench of putrefaction filled the room, beating back the aromas of the incense. I gagged. The man held the hand up to his eye and peered at me through it. He winked, but his expression was humorless.

He placed the hand below the proscenium arch of the girl's rib cage.

The woman and the man stood together behind the altar. They let their tunics fall to the floor. The man's chest was caved in and bruised, nipples like tiny black pebbles. The woman's breasts hung over a pregnant stomach. They put their hands on the grisly planchette, gestured with their eyes for me to join them. I did. Their skin was cool—the cold of the dead hand imbued everything with a growing chill.

The man cleared his throat to speak, and instead his knees buckled. He grabbed the side of the table and a series of hoarse sobs wracked him, veins standing out on his neck. The woman stroked his head, leaned over, and whispered into his ear. He straightened.

"Are you here, Carolyn?" he said, his voice trembling, breaking. The streams of smoke from the incense curled into ribbons. They shimmied in the dim light of the chandeliers. The curled dead hand shook and shivered and slid over to YES. The man gasped. He looked at the woman, his eyes wide. "It's working. It's actually working."

"Focus, Nicholas," she said, her eyes wide. "I'm not sure how long she can stay on this side."

Nicholas nodded, blinked back tears. He cleared his throat. "Tell us," he said. "Please—tell me what you see?"

The dead hand grew warmer. It began to swell. A split appeared in the skin, revealing yellow fat with brown striations. The three of us yanked our hands away when it got too hot to touch. The hand twitched. The fingers rubbed against one another. It slid over to NO. Then it flew around the letters, but too quickly to read, the rapid-fire rant of a madwoman. A blue and powdery mist came off the body as the hand flew from letter to letter. It formed a twister and then dissipated into the air.

The tattoo began to fade, and in its place bulged the features of a large and screaming face.

"That is not Carolyn," screeched the old man.

A high-pitched scream tore across the room. It was the woman. Black splotches had begun to form on her forehead. They rolled down her face like tears of ink. New lines sprung from a beauty mark on her cheek, swirling like vines around the vertical lines. Acrid smoke poured out of the lines and swam to the ceiling as she fell to her knees. She looked up at me, her breath coming in terrible howls. Her eyes began to sizzle in their sockets, and then they burst, spraying like milk. I turned to run and the man stood before me. His eyelids blackened and withered as though eaten away by invisible fire, his eyes bursting just as the woman's had. He opened his mouth to speak, and his teeth exploded into powder, forming a cloud of white around his head. Wounds appeared on his tongue as though it was being strafed with fire from a miniature machine gun. Thin black lines burst across his forehead like a spider's web and ran down his face like tears, pinpricks of black spreading out from them like magnetic filings, pimpling his face. He made a terrible gurgling noise.

I ducked past him and hit the door running. It was only after I bounded down the hall and burst into the stairwell, after I took the stairs four at a time, my breath bursting in shouts from my lungs, only once I collapsed on the beach near the tidal pools and the concrete steps, that the revelation came to me...that of the details I had missed in that frenzy of blood and smoke—the face that bulged from the torso of the dead tattoo was a face I'd known. And I'd recognized the lines that had torn apart the faces of the man and the woman, the thin lines, the intricacy. It was not Carolyn—she was gone, her suffering done. No, it was Pete who had been summoned that night, Pete who took his bloody revenge.

***

It was that night, ten years ago today, that I fled Hulse. If you'd known me back then, you wouldn't recognize the man who addresses you now. The holes from my piercings have closed. I'm clean-shaven, gaunt but pot-bellied. I dress in whatever Walmart throws onto its discount racks at the end of each season. I live in a two-room apartment, no posters on the walls. I go to my temp job in a featureless high-rise. I come home. I eat take-out and watch television that numbs my mind until I fall asleep. Every morning I check the mirror. The black spot under my right eye, which I discovered in my rearview mirror on the road out of Hulse, has stayed the same size. Until this morning. It may have elongated, just slightly. The discovery sent a jolt coursing through my body. For the first time in a long time, I spoke to Pete. I talked to him all day. *Remember hanging out at the shoreline, Pete? You bobbing out past the breakers, making fun of me for not daring to wade in past my ankles, me digging up mussel shells with my toes and looking out at the distant lights of Boston? Drinking on the rocks, flicking our cigarettes into the cove? What you must have thought, seeing me in that room. Please forgive me, Pete. Please spare me. I never had a choice.*

THE BURNT SUGAR STENCH

WENDY N. WAGNER

I couldn't tell how long the man in the black jacket had been slapping my face—except I knew my face hurt a lot, and that suggested a lot of slapping. I pushed myself upright on jelly arms, my head scraping on a wall too rough to be my apartment. For that matter, it was raining. It didn't rain in my apartment.

"The fuck am I?"

"You awake now?" The man gave me another slap. "Come on, Takas."

Maybe he was a cop. Cops were always calling you by your last name, like my middle school vice principal. I giggled a little at that.

"What the hell are you on?" He yanked my arm. "We got to get out of here."

I pulled free and let my arm fall back to my side. At least I was wearing a jacket, the new pink Columbia raincoat my mom had sent me for Valentine's Day. She never bought sweets for holidays, understandably. I licked my lips, still tasting of the future and artificial cherries. "Go away."

He grabbed my arm again and hoisted me to my feet. "Come on, Takas. We don't have much time."

A shot echoed down the alley, and the pieces of the present fell into place around me, and I let him half-carry me to his car. If he was a cop, I needed his help.

***

You'd think law enforcement would be more interested in the services of a twenty-year-old clairvoyant, but my biggest customers were organized crime. The Raskolnikovs kept me pretty much on retainer. I used to work with a few other gangs before the war dried them up, but since high school I've been exclusive to the Russians. They didn't seem to mind scheduling their sessions around my classes at PSU.

They came to do business at my studio apartment. I could have rented a space somewhere else, but in my line of work, there wasn't much point. They'd find me if they wanted to. Even if I went fully off-grid, there were still other fortune tellers who could find me if they really tried. And they would try. Being the best meant stepping on a lot of toes.

The cop must have known something about my work. He kept giving me little side-glances as he drove. The city looked different from the inside of a car, instead of on foot or from the steamy confines of public transit. The Central Eastside Industrial District looked edgy and hip, the bums tucked behind alleys too small for a Ford Taurus. You couldn't even smell the river in here, the dank mud-stink of high water. I let my head fall back on the headrest, every muscle jellied from what I'd been working on back there in that alley.

Had it worked? I squeezed my eyes shut, trying to remember what happened when I touched my fingers to the white sheet of space-time, hiding the future in its folds.

"Why do the Raskolnikovs want you so much? And why is the Del Rios gang after you?"

A faint accent hid inside his vowels. I hadn't noticed that back in the alley. I gave him another looking-over. With the future peeling back from my eyes, I could appreciate his cheekbones and long eyelashes much better. If he wasn't an import model, his parents were.

"What's your name?"

"What?" He stared at me for a second. "Aguilar. *Detective* Aguilar."

"Your mom named you 'detective'?"

"We don't have time for you to play cute. I've got a missing girl in a shipping container set to blow, and at least two witnesses claim you know where she is. We've got less than an hour to save her and stop a gang war that's gonna rip apart this city. So start talking!"

"Missing girl." I could see the video in my mind's eye, the girl tied to the stool, her blond hair no longer set in beauty pageant curls but only hanging limply around her bruised face. The Raskolnikovs had made me watch it fourteen times. "Rayna Raskolnikov." In the video, a digital clock sat about a foot away from the stool, its red digits running toward midnight.

"Yeah. The Raskolnikov heiress."

He stopped at a light, staring at me. I looked back at him, and saw lightning flicker on the other side of the driver's side window. Black lightning, as apocalyptic as a nuclear strike.

The fog in my head cleared. I was moving into the future now, and the past was starting to make sense. Whatever I'd set in motion before, I hadn't finished it.

"I'm going to need candy," I said. "Lots of it."

***

I grabbed one of the baskets sitting beside the front door. I was probably the first person in the history of this Plaid Pantry to ever use one. The clerk even put down his copy of *Guns and Ammo* to watch me head into the candy aisle.

Aguilar stepped around me. "What's this about?"

In the corner of my eye, the beer cooler bulged and flexed. A bottle of Zima exploded on the shelf. Aguilar shot it a confused look and turned back to me, his hand closing on my arm. The signs I'd seen hadn't told me the end of the world was going to come this fast.

I swallowed down guilt. Imagine destroying the world to make drug dealers a few more bucks. That's what I'd done, me and every fortune teller in Portland.

I shook off Aguilar's grip and pulled every package of Warheads off the rack. "Check the fruit candies. Anything super sour is a contender." I snatched up the last Sour Patch Kids package. "There. Special edition Skittles."

He picked up one package. I pushed him aside and grabbed up the other three packages in the case. Another box was tucked behind them; I took the whole thing.

If I was at home, I'd go straight for the pure stuff, but we didn't have time to head back to East County. I cut over to the drinks case, looking for the funny little bottles marketed for eight-year-old boys. There was always something, usually a blue lemonade or fruit punch packed into something with a shark's head for a lid. I turned over a bottle shaped like a grenade. Malic acid sat proudly as the third ingredient. I took two bottles.

"You got cash?"

"I can use my debit card." He handed the basket to the checkout guy, who looked from Aguilar to me and back again. I could see the judgments going back and forth like ping pong balls behind his eyes: tweaker, john, college student, pornographer. None of them added up, not with my nerdy glasses and Aguilar's general atmosphere of stick-up-the-ass.

"What are you waiting for?" I snapped. "And yes, we'll need a bag."

He offered the bag to Aguilar, and I snatched it out of his hand. Took a second of fumbling to find the grenade drink and then downed it as we walked out the door. The malic acid hit the hinges of my jaw like a burst of porcupine quills.

We got back in the car. I opened the first packet of Warheads.

"I'm gonna be in the future soon," I explained. "It'll be messy, but I need you to just keep driving. Go wherever I tell you." I wished I didn't need to chew the sticky stuff, but it made the acid enter my system that much faster.

My stomach churned around the candy. I hadn't had much real food the last two days, not since the Del Rios had issued their ultimatum.

"It's not drugs," I explained. "It started out that way, I guess, but then the Raskolnikovs started going to fortune tellers. You ever notice how many fortune tellers Portland has?"

Aguilar didn't answer. Could a man like him believe me? He looked ordinary enough, his clothes middle class, his haircut better than Supercuts. People above the poverty line didn't see the gang wars the rest of us did.

But he was a cop. He had to have seen the changes and wondered what caused them.

"I don't know what it is, but the Portland metro area has about twice as many fortune tellers as your average town. Palm readers, tarot readers. Clairvoyants like me. And more than a quarter of those diviners are the real deal."

"Sure." The disbelief dripped off his voice.

I ripped open a packet of Skittles. "Gang violence has changed, hasn't it? How often has Portland registered a drive-by or a street fight? It was zero last year, wasn't it? That's because of us. Because we looked into the future and told people where to be to cut off shipments of drugs and guns. We told people where there'd be a police sting or a rival ambush. We fortune tellers, we served the drug dealers—but we made this city safer."

His eyes flicked toward my face and then back to the view out the window. He kind of wanted to believe me. Of course he did. It's human nature to hope divination works. Why else do people keep going to astrologers and buying tarot cards? Every single member of our species is desperate to push back the folds of time and see what's waiting for them.

"The Raskolnikovs swallowed up the rest of the Russian street gangs," I explained. "Mostly because of my mother. Before she got out of town, she was their chief seer."

"What happened to her?"

Prescience twinged someplace in my gut. "Get on the freeway up here." I shifted in my seat, trying to get comfortable again. I remembered his question. "Diabetes."

"If she ate like you, I can see why."

"It's the malic acid," I explained. "For us, it pierces the veil between this time and the next."

A wave of it ran over me, the world disappearing behind a fog. The shipping container. It sat on the edge of an empty lot, black-berry vines growing over the back half. The debris of an abandoned homeless camp lay in heaps around it. Could have been anywhere in the outer ring of Portland streets—anyplace out of sight of the core where rich people nibbled avocado toast and tourists stood in endless lines for ice cream—but the lights behind it told me enough to make a decision.

"She's off Sandy someplace. Not too far from the airport."

"If you're lying, you'll be spending a long, long time in jail," he warned.

"It's true. We just have to find her in"—I checked the clock—"twenty minutes."

He spun the wheel harder than he needed, sending me sprawling against the Taurus's door. The east side flew by on either side of us, the quiet lights of the Parkview neighborhood a soft blur. I had grown up out here, grabbing donuts at Annie's with my friends, taking the bus to the pool over on Glisan. I had always felt safe. My mom would look into my future every morning and give me explicit directions to keep me out of danger. I wished she was here now, her soft bulk welcoming me to rest my head. If she was here, I could step away from all of this and just go do my calculus homework.

But she was two hundred miles away from here, working at a new age bookstore in Ashland, a slender version of herself that neither of us had ever seen in her future. She had begged me to come with her. Southern Oregon University didn't suck. I could graduate from there just as well as Portland State.

But of course, I couldn't. If I had gone to SOU, the world would already be over. The thing about Portland having twice the number of fortune tellers meant there were twice as many people fiddling about with space-time, pushing holes in the fabric to peek through. And once the Del Rios and the Raskolnikovs realized their power depended on a constant view of the future, the fortune telling business stopped spending their time luring in rubes with incense and love potions and started spending more time actually looking into the future.

The bad news is that space-time isn't as resilient as we thought it was. It only looked like a sturdy brocade, hefty curtains like the ones your grandmother bought to block out the view of the neighbor's house. The fabric of space-time is closer to gauze, flimsy and delicate. And what lay on the other side of it was far more dangerous than a bad view.

I reached for the second bottle of the malic acid grenade, even though I desperately didn't want to. Looking into the future risked making the holes in reality bigger, but doing nothing wouldn't stop the unraveling.

"So what? You're looking into the future right now? Do you see us saving Rayna?"

"I've been seeing what happens if she blows up. I saw it a year ago, because it's the nexus of all of this. If I'd been able to work for the Del Rios, I would have begged them not to take Rayna. The Raskolnikovs have put every fortune teller in the metro area to work finding her, and it's a disaster."

"Why?" The curiosity on his face was real. He was no longer

playing along. Somehow I was reaching him.

There was a convenience store up ahead, and something about its sign looked uncomfortably familiar. I opened another bag of Warheads. "Do you know what happens when I look into the future? When any clairvoyant looks into the future?"

"What? Oh, shit, what's wrong?"

The shakes were so powerful I had to grab the dashboard to stay upright. The future fell over me so thickly I couldn't even see the street ahead. "Turn left."

He began to slow the Taurus. But if we passed this turn, we'd never get back to Rayna. Never.

"Left! Now!"

A horn screamed. The car's wheels hit the curb and we rocked, hard, and for a second I thought our momentum would flip us over. Death breathed stickily down my neck.

And then we were safe on the shittiest road in all of northeast Portland, the pavement barely a memory, the gravel beneath more pothole than surface. Even though the only light came from the blue security light over the convenience store's dumpster, I could see enough to know we'd found the place.

"That's it."

Aguilar pulled up into the lot, the lights of the Taurus playing on the face of the boxcar. A heavy-duty chain secured its door, the metal the only shiny or clean thing in miles. A car pulled in behind us, one of those sleek little models gangsters liked for street racing. Aguilar reached for the gun in his shoulder holster. "You stay in the car."

I grabbed his arm. "No, it's not—"

Safe, I meant to say, I think, but the explosion rocked the Taurus so hard my seatback slammed the air out of my body. Aguilar's head hit the steering wheel and he slumped forward.

I reached for my seatbelt. A smell like scorched cotton candy filled the air. This wasn't the explosion Aguilar had been worried about: we still had seven minutes before the timer on the C4 in the railcar was set to blow. This explosion was something else entirely. This explosion was mine.

I got out of the car.

"Stop!" a voice shouted. I ignored it. All I could see was the woman waiting for me in front of the shipping container.

A shot resounded, loud enough to make my ears ring, and a bullet ricocheted off the shipping container's door. The woman beckoned to me with one knobbed finger. I took a step toward her. I figured I had about five minutes to fix all of this before time itself stopped existing.

Gunfire sounded behind me. I could hear Aguilar bellowing something, but I didn't pay him any attention. I couldn't stop staring at *her*.

A white bob framed her round, only lightly wrinkled face. Red-framed glasses, hipster huge, were more chic than geek. She wore a black linen dress that could have come straight out of the J. Crew catalog.

"You're a lot classier than I expected," I admitted. "And not nearly as chubby."

She rolled her eyes as she reached for my hand. It felt strange to be holding hands with my future self. Her fingers dug into mine as we both craned back our heads.

The fabric of time hung in shreds above the boxcar. A luminous blackness protruded through the gaps, ribbons of lightning crackling and hissing. Something moved between bolts of lightning, something whose pincers clicked and clacked like an army of spiders.

"Takas! What the hell are you doing? And who's the old lady?"

Aguilar ran past me, gun in one hand, bolt-cutters in the other. He didn't see the horror hanging over his head.

"Just get the girl!" one of me shouted, or maybe both.

Thunder sounded loud enough to vibrate my heart inside my chest. He was already fighting with the bolt cutters.

The *thing* began to crawl out of the black. Its claws tore at the

ribbons of time, tearing at the fabric of reality, widening its pas-
sage. Behind it, its kin screamed and hissed encouragement. Reality had held them back for eons, and we stupid fortune tellers had
invited them in.

And I was the worst of them. The strongest of them. I'd almost
single-handedly ended the gang wars simply by giving the Raskolnikovs so much information no one could compete with them.
After I'd had my first vision of this railcar blowing a hole into
space and time, I started looking for ways to fix things. But nothing I did helped.

So I did the most dangerous thing someone like me could do:
reached through the veil of the future and begged myself for help.

No wonder Aguilar had found me passed out in an alley. The
explosion over the shipping container was just one small manifes-
tation of the energy I'd used—I was lucky I hadn't killed myself.

Future Me dug her fingernails into my skin, pulling me out of
my pity party. Her free hand raised a mesh bag.

"We'll need this!"

She had to shout to be heard over the thunder and the screeching. The door to the shipping container stood open, and I could
see Aguilar doing something with the explosives sitting behind
Rayna Raskolnikov. Some of the screeching came from the girl. I
could hear sirens in the distance, and maybe gunfire.

I wrenched my eyes back to the mesh bag. The bottles inside
were actually glowing, the liquid a seething yellow like a bad
dream. She tossed me one. The lid was, of course, shaped like a
shark.

As one, we tossed back the super-sour drink. The malic acid
threatened to rip my jaw off my face, and capsaicin burned along
with the sour. My mind shot out the top of my head, slamming
into my future self's and twisting into a braid of power.

Our energy, phosphorescent yellow, shot out at the purple claw,
still hacking at space-time. Chitin snapped. The creature screamed,
its pain echoing through the world in waves of shock and terror.

Its voice was a color: a purple nearly ultraviolet. My body, barely connected to the thinking part of me, clutched at my eyes as they burned and stung from the hideousness of the light.

"Come on," Future Self yelled in my ear.

But I couldn't move. I could only stare around me, blinking in pain. A man screamed as the creature's blood, black and putrescent, rained down, searing his flesh. Aguilar must have handcuffed him to his own racing car, because now he hung from his wrist as the scorching goo spilled over him. His flesh began to smoke and sizzle.

"Come on!"

Fury spurred me back to work. We threw ourselves against the tear in space, our minds now yellow metaphysical hands seizing the torn fabric of time itself. The thing threw its weight against the gap, straining against our strength.

My future self growled. Her physical fingers dug deeper into my physical hand. Our metaphysical body grew brighter, and the sides of the tear began to pull together.

That's when the face appeared. An eye, a single eye burning with hate and entropy and the cold of an entire life spent outside the sphere of reality. I'd never felt such emptiness, such horrible hunger. I could feel it drinking up my feelings, my memories, my very existence. My grip loosened.

"No!" Future Self wailed.

Aguilar gave a shout of fear, and I saw him standing at the entrance of the shipping container, cradling the gangster heiress in his arms. A purple arm shot out of the sky, closing on Rayna Raskolnikov and hoisting her above the ground.

"Aguilar!" I screamed.

He pulled out his revolver and fired a full six rounds into the sky.

It couldn't have done anything. It *shouldn't* have done anything. But perhaps it simply startled the thing, or perhaps Aguilar's sheer anger and courage overwhelmed the part of it that fed on our powerlessness and fear. But it dropped Rayna and pulled back a little, and just like that, we were back in the game.

This time there was no straining. My selfs' yellow metaphysical hands drew the edges of space-time closed with the grind and screech of curtains closing over a dirty window.

Future Self dropped my hand. "You know what to do?"

I nodded.

"Give me a boost!" she ordered Aguilar, and even though he didn't understand what the hell she wanted, he lifted her so she could grab onto the roof of the boxcar and pull herself up.

Wind still streamed from the rip in the veil of time. It stirred her hair around her face and tugged on her linen dress. The black glow of the other reality lit up the scene like a malevolent black light. The burning yellow of our mental hands stained her hair the shade of Mountain Dew.

"Stop fucking around with time," she shouted down at me. "And go visit your mom!"

I wanted to wave, but she was already leaping at the gap. She floated for an instant and then the hole in space-time swallowed her up. Yellow crackled. Reality gave one last, ear-shattering sonic boom as it slapped back on itself. I fell to my knees, covering my ears, hugging my chest. The boom resounded inside every bone of my body.

The rain on the back of my neck finally got me to sit up. I wiped at my nose and realized the warm wetness was blood.

"Hey, are you okay?"

Aguilar knelt beside me. The blood vessels in his right eye had all burst.

I nodded.

He glanced at Rayna, lying still in the blackberry vines. Smoke rose from her body where the thing had touched her. The air stank of burned sugar.

I ran to her side. She looked so tiny like this. So many people had spent so much of themselves to find her. I dropped to my knees and felt for her wrist.

"Is she alive?"

I pressed my fingers into her wrist. "Please, Rayna. Please." *I'd* spent so much, trying to find her. I didn't know her, but I didn't want anything bad to happen to her, either.

Sirens sounded all around us. Aguilar put his hand on my shoulder.

"Takas."

I waved him away. "I'm still looking for a pulse."

"Takas!" He yanked me to my feet. "She's breathing. Look."

I sagged against him. "Oh, thank goodness. Thank goodness."

He put his arm around me and led me back to the Taurus. Without his help, I might have collapsed.

Holy shit. I had pulled my own future self through time to help fight off invaders from another reality. I'd sewn together a hole in space-time with the power of my own brain. No wonder I was tired.

"Do I even want to know what happened just now?" He opened the car door and I nearly fell inside. "I mean, were there really two of you fighting an unspeakable spider-monster hanging out of the sky?"

"You knew that was me?"

He sank into the driver's seat. There was a burn on his cheek like a smudge of raw purple. "Who else would wear glasses like that?"

I closed my eyes. "Wake me up when there's real food," I managed to whisper.

I think after that he said "Thanks for saving the world," but by that time, I was already mostly asleep, and dreaming of anything but sour candy.

WORSE THAN DEMONS

SCOTT R JONES

[*New Heretic Magazine*
[Asha Satyamurthy interview with Gregory Martens
[excerpt running time 00:23:17
[burstcast to noönet 20430215

New Heretic Magazine: A large part of your appeal as an *auteur* has been attributed to what some have called an obsession with the infantile. I'm not sure that's an entirely fair descriptor, but there is a marvelous sense of wonder in your films that could be called childlike. Can you tell us a bit about that?

Gregory Martens: Yeah, infantile, there's a rather obvious sneer in there, hey? Well, if it makes them feel clever, why not? Sure, I've never been afraid to explore the pre-verbal states in my work. I think, and I believe this, I really do, I think that we don't know what we are, as a species, because it's been so long since we were authentically ourselves. I mean, we were talking about memetic colonization the other day, Colleen Davros and I, this was up at Esalen for, what, Tusk's little think tank, and I said well sure it's an epidemic *now* but that's only because our ontological immune systems have become so fucking *compromised* by language in the first place, right?

NHM: That's nothing new, though, surely? Language as a virus? Burroughs and company made excellent hay of that idea seventy years ago.

GM: Absolutely, and it continues to agitate the infected to this day! More so, even. The uproar at Esalen, well. There's video, I encourage you to pull it up for shits and giggles. Before Tusk gets it pulled. Which, y'know, it's funny, it *is,* because I can recall years past when the idea would barely elicit a nervous cough or two from the audience. Colleen and I had to be escorted out for safety reasons. Now, why do you suppose *that* is?

NHM: It's a sensitive issue for a lot of people. The plague.

GM: Yes. And there's that fine old word, again. Fairly drips with associations. Sticky. Yes, *plague* tends to divide folks, historically. I'm going to correct you, though: It's a sensitive issue *to the virus.* But you wanted to talk about the films. I think it all comes down to, I don't want to say a return to Eden or anything like that, but certainly a reassessment of a childlike worldview, a pre-verbal worldview. I'm interested in seeing things as they *are,* or at least going as far as possible towards that. I don't think I succeed. I doubt I ever will.

NHM: Can you talk about projects where you've come close?

GM: That really depends on the mood I'm in? Mood factors quite heavily, because, again, pre-verbal knowledge, or aware-ness. And my mood today, well…open? Not exactly nostalgic, but there's a breeze from the past I've been feeling since I, since I woke up, really. Odd. But there again, trying to English it makes for the crumbling of the awareness. Ah, it's gone. Hey hey! Poof.

NHM: Sorry? Didn't want to throw you off.

GM: Oh, how can you be? I mean that sincerely. Proust had to swallow that cookie eventually! Don't worry about it. But sure, the films, the close ones. I'd say, today, *Headless,* that's definitely in the top five for me. Right this minute.

NHM: From your *All Along the Watchtower* trilogy.

GM: That's right. Well, by now most people know the ugly facts about my upbringing. No need to dirty ourselves up in the muck of that.

NHM: You were raised in a Jehovah's Witness church, yes.

GM: I was, I was, but god, don't let them hear you call it a *church*. You want to talk about groups with control language! Ah, but I'm being unfair, they all have it, to a greater or lesser degree.

NHM: They?

GM: Humans. In general. Religious groups, specifically. Cults, *especially*. So, with the J-Dubs, you had *The Kingdom,* and the *Little Flock. The New System. The Thousand Year Reign.* And of course, *Jehovah,* which they run into the ground, because God's gotta have a name. "We're the only ones who use it!" they shout, and I'm like, *yeah,* about that. It's lost on them, though. Shit, there's others, deeper, weirder. *Gog and Magog.* I find it odd and also comforting that I can't recall most of them, just now. But then, it's been a long inoculation process for me. Decades. I've been out of the Tower longer than I was in, really.

NHM: Not so out that they don't feature in your films, though?

GM: Never that far out! *Headless* perhaps being the best example. I wanted to explore themes of identity loss, fluidity, fragility, and the formative power of meaning, and the JW urban legend of the headless man kept suggesting itself to me as a framework for that.

NHM: Maybe I'm too much the unregenerate pagan to really understand this, but it surprises me that they'd have anything like that in their faith culture. Ghost stories?

GM: Oh honey. Honey, there's the letter of God's Law, and then there's the Spirit, and the Spirit gets around. Wants what it wants. Demonic Smurfs? Check. Angels guiding the good brothers or, more often, sisters away from houses where murderers, rapists, *worse,* wait behind the door? Check. Consider the risks they take, just walking up to random houses, knocking away with their clean white knuckles. Possessed garage sale items. Haunted macramé. Anyway. *Wayne,* which is what I called him in the film, because, y'know, Wayne. The headless man.

It's got all the classic elements, present in every version, and there are a few. So, the run-down area; if there are tracks in town, this house is on the wrong side. The rusted-out hulks up on blocks in the overgrown yard. Sagging roof, boards missing on the steps, paint peeling, garbage piled up in the driveway. Maybe throw some sun-bleached plastic toys in the yard for extra pathos.

Our two brethren approach, all clean and spit-polished, smiles bright, cheap book bags stuffed with copies of *Awake!* and *The Watchtower.* This house is never occupied, they know, or if it is the knock is never answered. This morning, there's music coming from inside, though. Something muted and heavy, so pick a metal band, something the audience will recognize as obviously Satanic but nothing too obscure. I mean, don't go with prog or Norwegian doom or anything like that. The brothers knock.

In some versions, a kid opens the door. The more feral and haunted looking the better. In others, it just swings open on a single hinge. In all versions, they're greeted with an interior that, to the average JW, fairly screams "Unclean! Unclean!" The music, obviously, now louder and more apparently Satan-friendly. The posters. Dungeons and Dragons paraphernalia. Drug paraphernalia. Kinky sex paraphernalia. Say a word often enough and it starts to sound dirty, have you noticed?

NHM: Paraphernalia. Paraphernalia.

GM: Parapher*nal*ia. Pair a fur nail ya. Yeah. It's less a house, more a museum to depravity. An object lesson.

NHM: Now, in *Headless,* when Wayne appears, it's played for laughs. Is that the case in the legend?

GM: Laughs? No. But their reaction to a clearly headless person isn't exactly natural. You or I, anybody, would tear out of there. Walking torso turns a corner and immediately begins begging for help, its voice coming from somewhere in the hazy air above its empty shoulders? Outta there. Right?

NHM: Of course.

GM: Not these two fine young Christian warriors. They know what they're seeing, and it is the Devil's handiwork, most assuredly. The demon which afflicts Wayne is mighty, it plays with his perception and the perception of others so that he only *appears* to be headless. *Naturally,* Wayne has lost his shipping clerk gig down at the pornography warehouse, his live-in girlfriend has left with the illegitimate kid or kids, he survives on rot-gut whiskey, Snickers bars and pot. He fears for his soul, his sanity and his life, in that order. And, y'know, hilarity ensues.

NHM: Did you have anyone else in mind for the role of Wayne? Or was it always going to be H. Jon Benjamin?

GM: He was top of my mind for the role, from the get-go. Only Benjamin could have given such personality to a faceless character. His early work is rough, but he really came into his own after the accident. Would that I could have worked with the original! A voice actor's voice actor.

NHM: Well, technically, the Benjamin we have is still the original Benjamin…

GM: His consciousness, sure. Resident on the noönet, like most things. I wonder if that's the same, though. As life. Living. I wonder about that all the time.

NHM: Speaking of dream projects…

GM: Ah.

NHM: *Spirit Board.*

GM: I've said it before. You *know* I've said it before. I say it every time that film gets brought up. Not a dream project, an *abortion.* From the start. And I could *swear* that was on the no-go list for this interview. I'm gonna kill my publicist…

NHM: *OK. OK.* I don't want to talk so much about the actual film. I hope that's all right, at least? Because that's been done.

GM: Uh-huh. To death. "The worst boondoggle since *Fitzcarraldo.*" That bastard Simek's piece in the *New Yorker.*

NHM: All the bad history and rumors of cursed sets aside, I'm more interested in the research you did in the year leading up to production on *Spirit Board,* which as everyone knows by now, was initially conceived as an autobiographical piece, a documentary. In particular, the trips you made to your hometown to interview certain individuals that…

GM: The Collingwood Five.

NHM: Umm…yes. The Five. Marlys Trachtenburg, Denny Fields, Craig Bender and Kavita Patel.

GM: And me. Greg Martens. See, this is why I don't like going here. I'm always the fifth. Asha, why not just come right out and put me at the head of the list? Why always the back end. Do you think I don't see it coming, somehow.

NHM: I'm sorry. I can see how this is uncomfortable for you. I think, and I'm only speaking for myself here as a journalist, I think I place you at the end of the list because you're the only one not in prison. I'm guessing it might be the same for other members of the press, too.

GM: Ahh, you're right. I'm being unfair. OK.

NHM: You're OK to continue?

GM: Yes. Yeah, sure. OK. Heh, there's that breeze again. It's like it's right in my face. Is my hair blowing back? Yeah, go ahead.

NHM: All right. Can you speak about the event that brought the Five together?

GM: Together? We were never *together,* not in the way you mean. We were kids. Craig was a seventh grader, the rest of us were in sixth. And I was never *with* them, not after the board. Not later, either, when the killings started.

NHM: They named you, though. The other four. They put you there.

GM: Yeah. I don't blame them for that. I *was* there. After all. I was a part of it, and a weird JW kid, too. So…

NHM: It must have been hell on your family.

GM: It was. I'll tell you, though, I think, on some level, they were proud of me. For doing the right thing. *The right thing* by some reckoning, anyway. For the publicity it brought the Tower.

NHM: Can you walk me through that morning?

GM: Understand, I was *eleven*. So were most of the people there. Who knows what we actually saw? It felt like a dream when it happened, and there are days I believe it was. I do. Some days I have to believe that.

NHM: It wasn't, though. Two teachers witnessed it, as well as the recess monitor. They testified, even. And the events afterward…

GM: Doesn't mean they weren't lying. Or believed the story enough to also believe it true. Doesn't mean they weren't dreaming with their eyes open. Or were affected by the, what did you call it earlier, the plague.

NHM: Babel Syndrome, yes.

GM: Yeah. Shit. No, you're right. I wish you weren't, that's all. Did you hear about that group in San Bernardino now? Cut out their tongues and speak only in emojis?

NHM: I have. Their membership is growing. Sales of personal holo-emitters are up. Personally, I think the literal speech bubbles floating above their heads is pretty cool. Like living in a comic book.

GM: Well, there you go. I might agree with you, too, if it weren't for the ritual mutilation. That's going to get worse, you know.

NHM: Can we get back to that morning? The Five?

GM: Right. Right. Well, there was the board. One of them had brought it. I think Marlys? She had a witchy, kinda hippy family, if I'm recalling correctly. Not that it matters who brought it. It was there. You can see these waves of interest in the occult surge through the popular culture. Youth culture. Have you noticed?

NHM: Sure. I sat on a panel once with an MIT guy who was convinced it happened on an eleven-year cycle that corresponded to sunspot activity.

GM: Seems legit. I mean, as anything else, really. So, y'know, kids had been trying that *light as a feather stiff as a board* levitation trick the week before. Other things. Who doesn't like a good scare. Marlys brought her Ouija board. Milton Bradley! What a

thing. Anyway. I stayed well away, being JW and all. Or tried to.
I was curious. Painfully curious. There was this big rock outcrop-
ping at the back of the schoolyard that we'd scramble around on,
and they'd set the board up there, Marlys and the other three. You
know how Ouija boards work?

NHM: Vaguely.

GM: It's like dowsing. When you dowse for water, or anything,
you hold the forked stick or a bent wire or a pendulum lightly, so
lightly, and then ask your question. You're not asking the spirits,
you're asking your own unconscious to access the flood of information that's always available to you but which gets reduced to
manageable levels by your waking awareness. Your body can feel
where the water is, you *know* it, on a deep level, but your waking
mind needs to receive that info from some other perceived source.
So the tiny fibers in your forearms and wrist and fingers twitch
and pull and nudge and hey, dig the well here, because guess what,
water. Or oil. Natural gas. I've dowsed for my car keys.

NHM: Do you find them?

GM: Every time. It's the same with the Ouija board. Hands
lightly rest on the planchette, and it moves across the board thanks
to the gentle push and pull of the players, movements that they
don't even *notice*.

NHM: So, the answers are pulled from the collective uncon-
sciousness of the players?

GM: Hm. Yes and no? There's a random factor to it, which is
why the early minutes of a Ouija session are almost always very
tentative and frustrating. Once you get into a groove, though.
Once the players get in sync.

NHM: Surely one player must dominate?

GM: You would think so, but no. Whatever comes through, it's
like Burroughs' Third Mind.

NHM: That would have been you then.

GM: No. No, I wasn't playing. I didn't ask any questions. The
Third Mind is generated by other minds in concert. If anything

I was the fifth mind, at the end. Small *m*. I hovered around the edges of the crowd. Like I said, curiosity. And there *was* a crowd. Not just kids, either. One of the teachers you mentioned. The recess monitor. It was theatre in the round, almost.

NHM: What kind of questions were the four asking?

GM: Oh, the old standards. Kavita and Marlys wanted names of boys they would marry. Denny was worried about his parents divorcing, wanted to know which one he'd end up with. It was Craig who started with the demon questions. Greasy little shit, Craig. He asked for names of demons that could hurt his enemies, scare his stepdad, make him rich, nothing more than that. He was twelve.

NHM: When were you brought in?

GM: Ah. The board did it. They did it, through the board. It asked a question of them and they decided I was the answer.

NHM: And that question was?

GM: "Who is the holy boy near?" Which could be interpreted at least a couple of ways. But see, I never swore. I didn't go trick or treating on Hallowe'en. And I had that squeaky smugness that young JWs have and never really get over. Stood out like a sore thumb. Craig signaled to his bruiser friends and before I knew it I was picked up by the armpits and flung to the ground in front of the four.

NHM: Where was the teacher during all this?

GM: She'd turned her head for a moment. The monitor, too. You remember the criminal stuff you could get away with if the timing was right. The moment was structured that way. And it's not like I yelled in protest or anything. I *wanted* to be closer, but I couldn't bring myself to do it. They wanted me to ask it something, and there was a threat of violence if I didn't. The whole scene was *charged*.

NHM: There's a similarly charged scene in *Spirit Board* that's spawned any number of theories. "The silent question." I've seen it ranked with Bill Murray's final whisper to Scarlett Johansson in *Lost in Translation,* and Monique Bledsel's chilling off-camera petition to the Pleiadian Intelligence in *Void Children.*

GM: I've read some of those. Interesting stuff. I'm glad it makes people think, but I...

NHM: What did you ask the board? That day.

GM: ...

NHM: Was it in fact a silent question? That later found its way into the film, or...?

GM: No. I spoke. I asked the board if it could tell me the name of God. Oh. Oh god. I just...Jesus. Jesus Christ.

NHM: Are you all right? Should we move on?

GM: No, I'm fine. I'm fine. It's...there's just so much happening now, I feel, I feel like everything is compressing down. Crushing. This terrible gravity to all our doings. Do you feel it, Asha?

NHM: Sometimes, yes. That's just the world, though. It's always been that way.

GM: You're young. That's nice. Nice, but wrong. I think you're wrong.

NHM: OK. Do we need to take a break?

GM: No. They answered me, through the board. Or the board did. Something answered. I'm not sure it was them, now. It was and it wasn't. Something came through. Heh. That's what they were always warning kids about, in the Kingdom Hall. Hell, any church of that type. Demons come through. They always come through.

NHM: May I hazard a guess as to the answer you received?

GM: Hazard away!

NHM: *Jehovah.* The name of God, or at least what you knew as the name of God. The kids, the board, spelled out *Jehovah.*

GM: Yes. And no. Not really. They spelled out the Tetragrammaton. Y H V H. *Yod Hey Vav Hey.*

NHM: The Hebrew name for God?

GM: The *ineffable* name *of* God. The *unutterable* name of *God.* Throw some vowels in there and you've got the bastardized *Jehovah* my old crew loved to toss around so much. The name I was familiar with. The name I knew and expected, in my smugness. I was gonna break that Ouija board, understand? Like a good Christian boy. Throw it a holy curve ball, right over the plate, set that board to spinning and cracking in half. Whatever was behind it was going to howl in terror and flee back to the dark. Like when Christ cast the demon Legion into a herd of swine and the piggies plunged off a cliff into the sea. Like when Wayne's head finally shimmered back into view after a few weeks of intense Bible study. Instead, I got letters I didn't recognize. And then the incident.

NHM: It wasn't the first outbreak of Babel Syndrome, but it was certainly one of the most dramatic. An entire school losing the power of speech? The Collingwood event pushed the health crisis into the national conversation.

GM: Oh, we had the power. We could *talk*. We just couldn't make ourselves *understood*. For weeks. It's why I made the fucking film in the first place. Why I don't trust myself with language when I make any film. And why I went to talk to the others, years later, after they did what they did. There was nothing to learn from them, though, nothing beyond what they'd already claimed in court. I think Craig enjoys prison. Denny and Kavita. Marlys. I dunno. They're hollowed out people now. There's nothing there but noise.

NHM: They say you exposed them to God.

GM: That sounds dirtier than it was. Or it's spot on. I don't know. Crazy people say things.

NHM: They say He made them do it.

GM: That old chestnut. That old *noise*. What's worse than the devil, Asha. What's worse than demons. Listen. Those letters, the Y H V H. It's not just a name, it's a principle of pure Being. Do you get what I'm saying? You're not supposed to sound it out, but when you do, when you *do*, shit, it sounds like breathing. *Yaahh* in *vaahh* out, *yaahh vaahh,* in and out. He, it, breathes the universe into being.

I spoke to a rabbi once, my producer on *30 $ilver Pieces* put me in touch with the old guy, and after he very patiently sat with me as I blubbered out my theories, he said that God "is the Source and Foundation of all possibility of utterance and thus is beyond all definite descriptions." How do you like that? Was that supposed to be a comfort?

NHM: Was it?

GM: Oh honey, fuck no. No, it wasn't. Because it doesn't explain how those stupid kids knew about the Tetragrammaton. I don't think they did. *I* didn't even know, and I was the good JW boy! I prayed to the thing every night.

NHM: Do you think God is responsible for Babel Syndrome?

GM: We don't know what we are, Asha. We don't. We talk and talk and talk and we don't know what we're doing. Language, it's already a kind of half-miracle. The weird fact that I can make certain sounds with my vocal apparatus, my monkey-mouth, and because our dictionaries happen to agree, you can hear these sounds and understand them, and reproduce them, and we blather on and on. We do it because it works. But it's bizarre. It's power. And it's *nothing* because all words are made up, all descriptors arbitrary. I don't mind telling you, this stuff makes me afraid. I'm afraid all the time these days.

NHM: Why?

GM: Babel. Babylon. It was a city in the Fertile Crescent. It's in the book of Genesis. Nimrod, the mighty hunter-king, and his tower, purpose-built to pierce the vault of Heaven. Do you know this story?

NHM: No. I was raised New Reformed Atheist.

GM: The post-Dawkins bunch. Yeah, they do good work. How nice for you. Well, I won't bore you with it then. I'm scared because I look around, and I see what we've done, and what we might yet do. I think about those tongueless in San Bernardino, and I think about H. Jon Benjamin living in a block of superconductive crystal a mile deep in the earth's crust with thousands of other wealthy ghosts. I think about the Collingwood Five and collective minds from Outside and murder. I think about how this interview will be burstcast directly to the noönet, and people will watch it in their dreams or on their phone, depending on how much they want to spend. Jesus! And that Ouija board, that ridiculous cardboard tech. That's never far from my thoughts, Asha.

And I wonder if we haven't gone and built another tower. And I wonder if that's the kind of project that might agitate an invisible disembodied lifeform that hides in plain sight, colonizing our minds and moving us according to its will.

NHM: You're talking about God.

GM: Yes. No. Good Bye. I don't know. I'm always afraid. I was told, from a very young age, that the fear of God brings wisdom. I thought I was over that. Thought I knew better, but now I'm not so sure. I babble on, afraid and wiser by the minute, while they speak in emojis to save their souls. What do their prayers look like, in those little bubbles? Milton Bradley. Am I wise, Asha? Do I seem wise to you? Because I'm very afraid. What's worse than demons?

NHM: I can't speak to that.

GM: Probably for the best.

THE EMPRESS AND THE THREE OF SWORDS

AMBER-ROSE REED

London welcomed me back like an old friend. Though the people I had met when last I was here were mostly still in attendance, I noticed straight away that whatever routine I had kept among my friends had not continued in my absence. Such a thing was of course expected. I arrived at a ghastly time, or so said Wilton, an unfortunate actor I had occasion to see on my second day back. He complained of a breach among those in his social circles, though he knew nothing of what had happened, and did not seem to care, except for the inconvenience it caused him. He glanced at his reflection in the window of my lodging, as though to make sure his expression matched his imperious statement. I imagine he lay on such a far edge of such a circle, the waves of the troubles to which he alluded barely wet his feet.

Through Wilton, of course, I had made the acquaintance of many of the people he spoke of so dismissively, people whose names are known to any who travel in artistic circles in London. I inquired about a few of them, but when hearing one woman in particular was still in residence, I insisted that he and I go that very instant to her home, which had been a haven of mine in times past. He agreed reluctantly, as it seemed she was in the middle of whatever split had so shaken Wilton's social milieu.

It was well after supper when we arrived at the lady's home in Chelsea. Lamps burned against the darkening sky, gray clouds like smudges hovering above us as we climbed the brick steps to the front door. I saw light flickering inside through the window facing the street, though the silver lamp I had admired when last I came was not in view. I straightened the lapels of my coat as I waited, and Wilton tossed the artful tumble of his thick black hair.

Gypsy opened the door. That was the name Wilton had given me when first I had met the lady. Since then, I had learned much and more about her, including her given name, but no one ever used it. She looked much as she had when I last saw her—ageless as ever, pixie smile in place, dark hair framing her face. The coat that cinched at her waist was gray, and the skirt that billowed below it was black. I was used to seeing her in color—oranges like the sunset, blues like the morning, not grays and blacks like the clouds and the sky at my back that night. There was a flush beneath her tawny skin.

If our presence was a surprise, she did not show it. "Come in, come in," she said, ushering us through the door, her brusque welcome nonetheless warm, and yet I felt something was wrong, even though her smile and her voice were all I'd come to expect from this most unusual lady. "Not much of a group expected this evening, I'm afraid," she said, leading us into her parlour. I inquired about her friends, a tiny couple whom everyone playfully called the Birds. Gypsy let out a huff of air, a scoff or a laugh, I could not tell. "Sad to say, one of the Birds flew south for the winter, and the other…" She trailed off as we entered the room.

A woman stood alone in the middle of the parlour. Glittering white beads danced down her pale blue dress, and a pink sash wound around her waist, tied and left to stream down her back. She wore a band around her head, but stopped short of the feather the ladies in France had so popularized over the last months. She flicked midnight eyes toward me, and then toward Wilton, and then focused back on Gypsy. Wilton drooped at the woman's lack of recognition of his dapper suit or his thick, handsome hair, and followed Gypsy's direction to her blue sofa. I believe she had intended on both of us sharing the seat, but Wilton flung himself upon it as a lady in swoon.

I perched on its arm. Gypsy offered no introductions. She settled herself on a plush cushion on the floor, as was her custom, and did Wilton the kindness of asking him about his recent play.

While he explained the travails of playing a madman on the London stage—a story which he'd told me at length the moment he stepped into my lodging earlier—I watched Gypsy's other guest.

As we had entered, she retreated from the center. Shelves covered with books, statuettes, and various gimcracks stood against one wall, and the woman had made her way toward it. The woman seemed removed, somehow, from the conversation, from the room, even. A strange thing to think about a woman whose hands were flirting with the idea of touch, but her fingers barely brushed a single item. It seemed to me that I knew her, or should have known her. That not recognizing her was a mistake I was bound to pay for, and likely sooner rather than later. I looked away, unnerved, and concentrated on our hostess.

"And what of yourself?" I interjected when Wilton paused for longer than it took to suck in a quick breath. "What have your endeavors been lately?"

I'd hoped she would tell a story, or perform a song, but it did not seem as though those projects were the ones on her mind. "Just finished a job," she said, and her forehead creased with a frown even though her lips barely twitched. "Very little money in it."

Her very reticence piqued my curiosity. "What sort of job?"

Gypsy's dark eyes left my face and went to the woman's. They seemed to speak without saying a word, their eyes locked across the room. The silence hung in the air, much heavier than the orange blossom scent from the incense burner near the window.

"A deck of cards," she said at last, returning her gaze to me.

"Playing cards?"

"Of a sort," Gypsy said, and rose to her feet. She retreated to the shelves in the corner and retrieved a red box, one of its corners already splitting at the seam. "Have you heard of the Tarot?"

I had, though only vaguely. Gypsy ran in occult circles, I knew, and there was some crossover with the artists, actors, and writers I had met in her parlour a few years ago. I asked for an explanation, but it was not Gypsy who gave me one.

"Divination is a useful way to learn the truth of oneself and the Great Work," the woman said calmly. "To find a path. Especially when we've lost ours."

Our hostess offered nothing further. She returned to her cushion on the floor, and tapped the bottom of the box, until a hefty stack of cards fell into her left hand. She fanned out the cards in front of her, the back of the deck facing up, white roses and lilies checkered on across a sea of blue. "Game of whist?" she asked with a little laugh.

I descended from my perch to sit before her as she shuffled the cards. And then, to my surprise, so did the woman, sitting beside me without care for her shimmering dress against the floor. Gypsy flashed a smile at both of us, though I dare to believe even now that the smile leveled at me was a fair amount brighter than that given to the woman. She took the cards in her left hand and dealt them out in the shape of a cross.

"The central card represents the one who seeks answers," the woman said.

"This is me, then," Gypsy replied, and turned the card. A dark-haired woman sat on a throne in an autumnal field, garlands of roses surrounding her. I looked from the card to the lady, and felt warmth steal into my chest. She was a queen, of sorts, a queen of the cloudland she opened to all of us. And queen and creator of the vibrant goldenrod and maroon world of the card below.

"How beautiful," I murmured.

"Great of spirit," the woman said, her voice wry, as though quoting.

Gypsy's brow arched, equally wry. "Or from your side, suspicion." I nearly asked what she meant, but stopped short of doing so. Gypsy turned the card that had laid across the Queen. "This is my obstacle." A red heart was emblazoned upon a tannish background, so bright I nearly expected it to beat. Three swords were plunged through the heart, silvery bright and familiar to me.

"Oh!" I exclaimed, leaning in to get a closer look. "Is that not the same sword you gave the Birds?" I had been in this very room when Gypsy had presented it for their use, pulled from the wall. I looked to where it had once hung, but there was nothing there, as though the Birds had never brought it back before mysteriously fleeing.

"The sword is the same." I looked up at her as she spoke, and caught the end of the look she leveled at the woman sitting beside me. Reproach lay in that stare, but I knew nothing of what had transpired.

The next card, she said as she turned it up, crowned her. The best of her intentions, she clarified. A craftsman at work, as I knew she always had been. The next card she turned up was beneath the central card, a hooded figure standing between overturned cups and ones still standing upright—what was inside of her, she said.

"This is behind me," she said, and turned the card up. A figure with a brightly colored cape walked away from a row of cups while a frowning moon looked on. The card gave me a feeling of inescapable sadness, more even than the one before, and I was glad it was behind her.

"This is before me," she said, and flipped the sixth card. A specter of Death loomed above a field of the prostrate. Above him waved a flag adorned with a white poppy.

Ghastly, I wanted to say, but did not. Was it there on my face to see?

"It is not as terrible as it seems," the artist herself said. "It is not

Death itself that comes before me."

"Then what is it?"

"Change," the woman said, lashes sweeping her cheeks as she closed her eyes. "Necessary, for survival."

"But change how?" Gypsy challenged. "Our interpretations guide us through the reading."

The woman conceded that with a tip of her head. "'When shall the stars be blown about the sky, like the sparks blown out of a smithy, and die?'" she quoted.

There were four more cards to turn. The first, on the bottom of the row, was the happy figure of an empress, bolstered upon pillows, in a field of gold and green. "Myself again," she said, both queen and empress. Gypsy moved immediately to the next one, which was an old Roman, his staff crowned with laurels—her environment, she said.

"This one holds my hopes and fears," Gypsy intoned, and turned the third card.

A man in a cap and trousers absconded with five swords, leaving two behind. It was brightly colored, cheering. "This symbolizes confidence and wishes. An attempt to create something new." Gypsy turned her face down, a smile flitting across it. "A plan that may fail."

This room had been full of life and light and color, but something recent had happened to dampen it all down, and I did not understand. Fingers had danced along ivory keys and voices had shook the tiny silver figurines all lined up atop the shelves, but now there was something blighted about this place. I felt, staring between the two women, that I would never know the answer, a thing I still believe to be true. What was it that had been left behind to blight that cheering face going forward?

"This last represents what is to come." Gypsy reached her hand toward the card. The tips of her fingers toyed with the edge of the card, then pulled away. She tapped two fingers against roses and lilies, and then pulled her hand away.

"That's not—" the woman began. She reached her own hand out, but stopped herself short of touching. Her body settled back and her eyes went back to Gypsy, eyes flashing an accusation.

"Perhaps I don't want to know the future," Gypsy said.

The woman stood abruptly. "You'll see it soon enough."

Gypsy made no comment on her exit. To my right, Wilton did not either. "Your friend has fallen asleep," Gypsy said. A glance confirmed it. When I looked back at her, her eyes were focused downward on the checkered back of the last card.

"You don't want to know?" I asked.

Gypsy looked up at me. Her eyes glittered in the warm yellow candlelight.

"I'll see it soon enough," she repeated, and swept the cards into a messy pile.

QUESTIONS AND ANSWERS

DAVID TEMPLETON

"**G**ood morning, people! You lucky, *lucky* people!"

Startled from silence, seven sullen recruits, each mutely hunkered around a large wooden table, all pop upright in their seats like slices of bread in a slightly rusty toaster. Turning, they watch as Doug, slender and bright-eyed, darts into the room, a stack of ancient textbooks clutched in his long, thin arms. With a hefty thump, he dumps the books on a small desk at the front of the room. Beside them is a neatly stacked pile of thick, rectangular boards.

He turns to face the class.

"All right, then!" says the young man, bouncing softly on his heels, his face brimming with enthusiasm. "Who's ready to *learn* something?"

Instantly, each member of the class reaches the same conclusion.

For a dead man, this guy is way too fucking lively.

"What can I say? I love being dead!" he says, smile widening, his voice as crackling with energy as an aluminum lunchbox crammed with electric eels. "And I *love* my post-death career! Let's hope the same will be true of all of you!

"Anyway...first things first!" he continues. "I'm Doug, assistant instructor. I've been dead...let's see, almost five years now. Wow!

Time flies! Hey! Want to know how I died? It was crazy! A refrigerator fell on me. My bad…total accident…shit happens. Anyway, I signed up for classes here as soon as I could after that. After I, you know, crossed over."

Doug stops, abruptly.

He's trying too hard.

He knows it.

"Okay…anyway…" he breathes out, forcing himself to slow down. "On behalf of the faculty here at Otherside University, I'd like to welcome you to day one of Elementary Occupational Spirit Board Training. This is room B-1. If you're looking for Second-Level Residence Haunting, which met in this room last semester, it's now down the hall, in B-6. Everybody cool?"

"Oh. Yeah. Definitely."

From the far left of the table, a youngish, redheaded, recently deceased mortician's assistant sits nodding…wondering to herself how anyone could be *accidentally* crushed under a refrigerator.

This guy must have been a real loser.

Unlike herself, who'd died of *cancer*.

Like a *normal* person.

"Spirit Board Training," she repeats. "Ouija boards. Yep. I'm in the right place."

"Awesome," Doug says. "Glad to hear it. Anyway, in this course, you will all learn the age-old mysteries of the spirit board, commonly called the Ouija board. Technically, of course, that's more of a brand name. Spirit boards actually *pre-dated* the Ouija by decades.

"Anyway, in this class you'll learn how to turn a board on, how to turn it off, and how to operate it from this side of the Veil…the *Great Divide* between life and death. Some of you might remember that… the Great Divide…that place you were floating in on your way to Otherside."

He pauses, all too conspicuously suppressing a deep shudder of emotion.

Apparently, Doug's memories of the Great Divide are far less than positive.

"Um, regardless of what most people assume over on Lifeside, the board is *not* as spooky as it seems," he says. "But actually, operating a board can be kind of dull and technical and tedious."

Doug notices that the faces of his class have turned from skepticism to concern.

"Not that it isn't still *fascinating!*" he adds, quickly. "I love how someone Lifeside can work out a question on the board, one letter at a time, and then, when we get the question over *here,* we get it *all at once.* There's even a *spell-check function.* On our side. So when we type out our answer and hit 'SEND,' they get it…properly spelled…*one letter at a time.*

"Yes, they have to *wait for it,* but it makes it *mean* more."

Doug smiles.

"Of course, there *are* rules. And there are consequences for *disobeying* those rules."

"Oh, stop it! You're scaring us," says Cancer Girl.

She turns to her classmates, smiling and rolling her eyes.

They do not smile back.

In fact, one of them, a middle-aged bartender killed by a drunk for serving a lemon twist instead of an olive, is clearly concerned, furrowing his brow into a knot of disconcerted worry. Another student—a former police officer run over by her own squad car when it slipped out of park while she was writing a speeding ticket—is nodding vigorously, ever the fan of following rules.

"Okay, before we go further," Doug continues, "I'm supposed to ask who you are—and what it is that interests you in becoming a spirit board operator. I mean, why not learn how to work Tarot cards? Why not *tea leaves?* Why not the *Magic 8-Ball?* And why take up the board now, at this particular stage of your afterlife?

"Also, if you care to share it," he goes on, "we'd like to hear how you died. That's optional, of course. Death is private stuff. But sometimes it can have a significant impact on how you function, or don't, as a spirit board operator."

For a long stretched-out moment, no one speaks.

"Can we actually take a class in the Magic 8-Ball?" Cancer Girl finally asks. "Can I switch to that?"

"Um, no," replies Doug. "The Magic 8-Ball isn't really a thing. It's just a toy."

"Well, isn't the Ouija board just a toy?" asks a short, muscular gentleman who was an insurance salesman, until he was toasted alive in a car accident. "I happen to know the Ouija board was originally patented, as a toy, in the late 1800s. Yeah, it's true, by a salesman named Elijah Bond. The patent was filed on the tenth of February, 1891. For years after that, the Ouija was thought of as a harmless parlor game, until World War I, when the American spiritualist movement rebranded it as a way to speak with the dead. Elijah Bond, by the way, had fought for the Confederacy during the Civil War. He's currently buried in a graveyard in the Green Mount Cemetery in Dorsey, Maryland. His gravestone is shaped like a very large Ouija board."

He shrugs.

"What can I say?" asks Toasted. "I was a two-time semi-finalist on Jeopardy."

"Ah. Congratulations. So, where are we?" asks Doug.

"We're about to share how we all died, and why we're here," says Cancer Girl. "We already know how *you* died."

"Yep. Refrigerator," says Doug.

"Nice." She smiles. "Me? I'm in this class because I'm more comfortable with the dead than with the living, and I figured, now that I'm officially deceased, maybe talking to the living would give me the same satisfaction that hanging out with the dead gave me when I was alive. Creepy but true. Oh, and…how'd I die? Garden variety Leukemia."

"Nice," says Doug. "Well, not *nice*, but…good! Good that you've started us off. Anyone else?"

"All right, I suppose I'll go," murmurs a small elderly woman seated beside Cancer Girl. "I drowned in my bathtub while having a mild heart attack. And I'm here because my P.D.A....my Post-Death Advocate...said a part-time job would be good for me. She says it might help me get over my P.D.D. You know, my Post-Death Depression. I've been pretty low. I miss having a purpose. My P.D.A. suggested Spirit Board Duty. Because I was a kindergarten teacher, and I'm used to working with people who read and write just one letter at a time."

"That's funny," chuckles Toasted. "You're very funny."

"Thank you. And one more thing," Bathtub Lady adds, clearly more than confortable with the topic of alphabets and writing. "I find it very odd that the Ouija board, presumably designed for people to ask questions on, does not include any actual question marks. Just letters, and some numbers, and the words 'Yes,' 'No,' and 'Goodbye.'"

"I know, right?" shouts Doug, excitedly. "The thing is, the living don't need a question mark, because when you get the message on your end of the board...the question mark is there anyway. Chalk that up to management efficiency!"

The ice now broken, everyone takes a turn.

Twist-not-an-Olive has enrolled because he's good at drunken late-night banter.

Officer Squad Car thinks spirit board operation sounds more interesting than working behind a desk at Central Spirit Processing, while Toasted signed up because he was bored with his last Otherside assignment working in the Reference Library of Lifeside Facts and Figures. The last two to share are another salesman, of sorts, who died when a competitor threw him from a high-rise, and a businesswoman-turned-actress, a devoted community theater fanatic, who'd fallen through a faulty trap door while rehearsing a death scene in an Agatha Christie mystery.

"I've always been clumsy," she blushes. "But I am extremely enthusiastic."

"What a promising group," Doug silently thinks. "They're all wounded, somewhat likable, and reasonably insecure. That's good. That's refreshing." A surprising number of spirit board applicants are freshly dead Internet trolls...angry people, overtly thrilled at the thought of using the Ouija board to fuck with people.

Such behavior is forbidden, of course.

In fact, this class was designed to identify and eliminate such applicants.

For decades...long before the Internet...the spirit board had been thought of all across Otherside as a sacred craft, one that had always been taught slowly by a spirit board master, one apprentice at a time. Bad apples would still slip through, obviously. There were countless stories of rogue board operators who abused the system, thinking it hilarious to make contact with the living and then falsely identify themselves as angry dead relatives, or demons, or seriously demented inter-dimensional entities.

They scared the shit out of people.

To prevent such abuses from happening, the spirit board course was designed. Strict rules were developed, severely limiting the choices that operators could make while operating the board. Around that time, the textbook was created.

"Hey! Refrigerator Guy! Now what?"

Cancer Girl, having silently moved over to where Doug is standing, touches him on the arm, gently attempting to break whatever reverie he's fallen into.

"Wow. Oops. Sorry!" he says. "Just...organizing my thoughts!"

Turning away, Doug makes a mental note that Cancer Girl is the first person who's physically touched him since he died...presuming, of course, that the word "physical" even applies in the afterlife.

"So...what's next?" Cancer Girl asks.

"What's next is...everyone gets a board, and a book!"

Quickly, Doug scoops up the stack of spirit boards on the desk.

"Hey! Um...I'm sorry...what's your name?"

"Rebecca," says Cancer Girl.

"Rebecca," nods Doug. "…Um, would you mind grabbing those textbooks?"

Following Doug's lead, Rebecca collects the stack of textbooks and, stepping a few paces behind him, sets one book directly on top of every spirit board Doug places before the waiting students.

"Excellent." Doug nods. "Have a seat…Rebecca."

"You're welcome…Refrigerator Guy," she replies, returning to her chair.

"Okay, do me a favor," Doug says, addressing the entire class now. "Don't open your books. We'll do that in a minute, I promise. First, it's the policy of the Boss…the primary instructor of this course…I'm just the assistant, right? It's the policy of the Boss that every new student be told the history of the Spirit Board Textbook *before* they open it. The Boss wants everyone to know exactly what happens…*what goes wrong*…when some new Board operator decides to improvise…to do their own thing…for, you know, *selfish reasons.*"

Officer Squad Car raises her hand.

"Is this the part where we find out what happens if we break the rules?"

"Exactly," Doug smiles. "This is *that*…the part where I tell you a story…a *true* story…a cautionary tale about breaking the rules."

"I always hated cautionary tales," murmurs Tossed-Off-a-Building.

"Me too," whispers Twist-not-an-Olive.

Doug takes a breath.

"So…has anyone here ever heard of Alice Cooper?"

Whatever it was the group has been expecting Doug to say next, this wasn't it.

"Alice Cooper…the rock star from the seventies?" he continues. "'No More Mister Nice Guy?' 'Welcome to My Nightmare?' That guy?"

"We know who Alice Cooper is," says Trap Door Accident, a slightly freaked-out expression scrawling itself across her face like a rude word on a chalkboard.

"Well, I've never heard of her," says Bathtub-Heart-Attack Lady.

"His real name was Vincent…Vincent Furnier," explains Doug. "There's an interesting urban legend about him. Supposedly, he chose his stage name…Alice Cooper…after consulting the Ouija board one night. The details vary, but supposedly he was in a hotel room in Tucson, Arizona, and one of his band mates had a Ouija board. They were still called The Spiders then, but wanted a new name, and everything they thought of was either not right or already taken. So, after different band members took a turn asking stupid questions, eventually, Vincent took a turn on the board, and asked, 'Hey Dead People! What should we name our awesome band?'

"After a short pause, the Ouija board began spelling out A-L-I-C-E and C-O-O-P-E-R. For years, he told that story, made a big deal of it. But in his sixties, after he'd become famous and started golfing with Pat Boone, Vincent switched course, telling people that the Ouija story was totally made up, that some fan invented it."

"So…that story's not true?" asks Twist-not-an-Olive. "Dammit! I must have told a million people that story. It was a total lie?"

"Well…let's call it a *half*-lie." Doug grins. "Truth is, Vincent really *did* get that name from the Ouija board. Only under slightly different circumstances than the ones he described."

With his well-practiced preface now complete, Doug takes a seat on the edge of the desk, and begins his story.

***

It was the summer of 1968, a few hours after midnight, Arizona time.

That was an especially busy morning out in the Otherside Spirit Board control room, where a brilliant, impulsive, slightly frightening woman, known to her fellow board operators as "Scary," had just returned from her lunch break.

It was near the end of her third full month on the job.

She wasn't happy.

Scary took a seat in her cubicle, plugged in her board, flipped the switches that connected it to the Great Divide, and tuned the board's frequency to North America, her designated "beat." After a moment or two, the spirit board began glowing blue. It gave out a soft, pleasant "BING!," the signal that someone on Lifeside had just been randomly directed to Scary's board.

It was from San Francisco.

A group of heavily tripping flower children wanted to know if there was really a god...and if so, was he or she interested in a four-way with them.

Scary wrinkled her nose, wryly. A number of colorful responses occurred to her, but instead of following those impulses, she obediently followed the textbook.

The textbook was very clear in regards to "spiritual questions."

Spirit board operators were forbidden to answer them.

So, Scary declined to answer the hippies from San Francisco.

Too bad, too.

She'd thought of a hilarious answer.

After a while, the blue faded, and Scary sat waiting for her next call.

She hated not being allowed to respond to an honest question. But there were a vast number of questions to which board operators were not allowed to give an answer.

The Big Three, as they were known around the Control Room, were the most common.

1. *"IS THERE A GOD?"*
2. *"WHERE WILL I GO WHEN I DIE?"*
3. *"HEY! WHO IS THIS?"*

The rules were very clear, though.

Never answer spiritual questions.

Never give any details whatsoever about Otherside.

Never identify yourself.

To Scary, it seemed cold and unfriendly, giving people the silent treatment like that.

Still, she recognized that silence wasn't necessarily a bad policy. Sometimes…actually, most of the time…*no* answer was better than a *bad* answer. In fact, in some cases, when no spirit board answer arrived from the great beyond, the Lifeside caller's own best instincts would kick in. Unconsciously, they would actually solve their own problem, gradually working out a fairly decent answer all on their own.

One letter at a time.

For instance, there was the time a young man named Bill, at the end of his rope following years of self-destructive addictions, consulted the Ouija, asking what steps he might take to gain a little control over his lifelong thirst for whiskey.

"NO MORE THAN TWELVE," Bill suggested.

Across the Veil, in the Command Center, as Bill's spirit board operator that night desperately flipped through the textbook, Bill grew impatient. Without knowing he was doing it, he reached down into his own better self, and soon, one letter at a time, had spelled out his twelve steps.

That worked out fairly well, all things considered, even if Bill did always believe those steps had come from some "higher power," instead of from the inherent human wisdom he unwittingly carried within himself.

Then again, on occasion, a caller's own original answers could be dreadful.

Once, in the early 1900s, a woman named Emily Grant Hutchins used a Ouija board to ask Mark Twain to dictate a novel, using her as his secretary. The operator on-shift that night also remained silent, for the simple reason that he was, in fact, Mark Twain. But Emily Grant Hutchins began writing anyway, and eventually produced a novel she proudly claimed had been dictated by the ghost of Mark Twain. It was terrible. So much so that Twain's estate promptly sued Emily Grant Hutchins for defamation of character.

Having heard many such stories over the course of her training, Scary knew there were serious dangers to almost any response a spirit board operator might give. The pressure of that knowledge could sometimes be crippling. To relieve that stress, the textbook contained pages and pages of common spirit board questions... with a large number of "management sanctioned" answers, each one spelled out clearly.

Occasionally, the answer was simply another question.

LIFESIDE: *"SHOULD I ACCEPT THIS JOB PROMOTION?"*
OTHERSIDE: *"WHAT DOES YOUR HEART TELL YOU."*

LIFESIDE: *"WHERE IS MY LOST DIAMOND EARRING?"*
OTHERSIDE: *"WHEN DID YOU SEE IT LAST."*

LIFESIDE: *"WHAT IS MY NAME, AND HOW MANY FIN-GERS AM I HOLDING UP RIGHT NOW?"*
OTHERSIDE: *"DON'T YOU HAVE ANYTHING BETTER TO DO."*

Actual *answers* weren't always much better.

LIFESIDE: *"WHEN WILL I WIN THE LOTTERY?"*
OTHERSIDE: *"WHEN IT IS YOUR MOMENT."*

LIFESIDE: *"AM I EVER GOING TO BE HAPPY?"*
OTHERSIDE: *"IF IT IS MEANT TO BE."*

LIFESIDE: *"SHOULD I JUST KILL MYSELF?"*
OTHERSIDE: *"UNCERTAIN AT THIS TIME."*

"Uncertain at this time."

Scary *hated* that one especially.

It was, according the textbook, the answer to dozens of questions, including the suicide question. It was why Scary hated suicide calls. That one single stupid phrase was all she was allowed to say. Nothing helpful. Nothing *true.*

Only, *"Uncertain at this time."*

That, or complete silence.

"BING!"

Scary's second call was from a young man in Portland, Oregon.

"IS MY MOM THERE?"

Fuck.

Scary hated that one too. And she got it a lot.

"IS MY MOM THERE?"

Or *"CAN I TALK TO MY HUSBAND?"*

Or, *"I JUST WANT TO HEAR FROM MY LITTLE BABY DAUGHTER."*

But the dead are *never* allowed to talk to their own loved ones.

That, everyone knew, could lead to a conflict of interest.

In the rare cases a spirit board operator received a call from someone they had known when they were alive, especially a person they'd loved, they were to step away from their cubicle immediately and summon the floor manager, who would call in a substitute.

So, that night, when Missing-Mom-in-Portland called up to speak to his mother, Scary followed the rules, and declined to reply.

Sitting there alone in her cubicle, thinking of that poor guy sitting in the dark, waiting, Scary's heart began to ache, knowing that she'd let the poor guy down…that she'd missed a chance to do some actual good in the world. Gradually, she started becoming angry. All this obfuscation and misdirection was not what she'd signed up for. She was told she'd be doing something positive with her death, making up for all the opportunities to help that she'd passed over when she was alive.

"BING!"

Yanked from her thoughts, her board glowing blue again, Scary saw that the next call was coming from a hotel room in Tuscon, Arizona.

She flicked the switch.

"HEY! DEAD PEOPLE! WHAT SHOULD WE NAME OUR

AWESOME BAND?"

Impulsively, she wrote out an answer and sent it.

"WHO GIVES A SHIT," she said, adding, *"AND STOP WASTING MY TIME…ASSHOLE."*

Scary knew she was engaging in a serious break in protocol.

She stood up. Time to take another break.

But before she could escape her cubicle, a second question popped up on the board.

"NO. SERIOUSLY. WE NEED A NAME. PLEASE?"

Scary stared at the screen. She was just reaching over to unplug the board, when *a third* question appeared.

"BY THE WAY…WHO IS THIS?"

"Oh, fuck it!" Scary sighed, aloud, sitting abruptly back in her chair. *"Let* them fire me."

Pulling the board closer, she typed out an answer and hit the button.

"ALICE COOPER," she said.

That was, in fact, Scary's real name.

Alice Cooper.

It was the truth. And right at that moment, Scary desperately needed to tell someone the truth.

Meanwhile, over on Lifeside, Vincent Furnier and his band were laughing their asses off.

"Alice Cooper."

Of course, they all took this unexpected suggestion as the answer to their *original* question. Vincent thought it was hilarious. In fact, he thought it was *perfect.* Fully appreciating the notion of a badass rocker, devoted to songs about nightmares, devils and black widows, with a stage name as sweet and harmless as Alice Cooper, he decided, right then and there, to change his name to Alice Cooper.

***

"The rest, of course, is history," announces Doug, finishing his tale with a wide smile.

"Oh, bull," says Rebecca. "You're shitting us."

"No. No I am not," replies Doug. "That really is how Alice Cooper got his name."

"And *that's* our cautionary tale?" asks Trap Door Accident.

"That's it." Doug nods.

"But…" states Tossed-Off-a-Building, "it's not cautionary. It doesn't have a scary ending."

"Well, Scary…Alice…*did* lose her job," replies Doug. "After the incident, she refused to back down, insisting to the end that telling the truth…using your instincts…is better than following rules you know are wrong. So they fired her. Basically—"

"Wait," interrupts Officer Squad Car. "So, the whole point of the story is…if we break the rules, we'll get fired? Why didn't you just say that?"

"Well…" Doug says. "There actually *is* one more *tiny* part. See, Alice *did* get thrown out, but by then she'd become kind of famous around here. Everyone knew she'd only done what a lot of spirit board operators had been too afraid to do. She'd told the truth.

"Then, one night, this one board operator, a former cabdriver, who'd fallen asleep at the wheel…and who'd known and liked Scary…he got a question from some stupid, heartbroken teenage guy. A girl he'd liked broke up with him on his nineteenth birthday. The kid was devastated. So he decided to go the Grand Canyon and walk off a cliff. Heartbreak Kid even bought a plane ticket to Phoenix.

"The night before his flight, he suddenly pulled out a Ouija board, a present from one of his stoner friends on his birthday. On a whim, he set it up, and sent a question out into the beyond.

'SHOULD I, OR SHOULDN'T I…KILL MYSELF?'

"So, of course, *that's* the question that Sleepy Cabdriver got that night. He knew the rules, though. He knew what the management sanctioned answer was to that question."

"Uncertain at this time?" asks Rebecca.

"Right!" says Doug.

"But he couldn't do it, could he, the sleepy cabdriver?" asks Officer Squad Car.

"No. He couldn't," Doug confirms. "He thought of Alice Cooper…the woman, not the rock star…and instead of sending *'Uncertain at this time,'* he sent the words, *'YOU SHOULDN'T.'* Then, inspired by Alice's enduring example, he added, *'YOU STUPID FUCKING IDIOT.'*

"The kid was stunned, to say the least," Doug says.

"WHAT DID YOU CALL ME?' he wrote back.

"FUCK WHAT I CALLED YOU. DON'T YOU DARE KILL YOURSELF!' Cabdriver wrote back. *STAY ALIVE! LIVE AS LONG AS YOU CAN. BELIEVE ME! BROKEN-HEARTED AND ALIVE IS A LOT BETTER THAN BROKEN-HEARTED AND DEAD! TRY GETTING OUT OF YOUR OWN HEAD FOR A WHILE. MAYBE TRY VOLUNTEERING FOR SOME CHARITY THAT HELPS POOR PEOPLE. THAT MIGHT HELP YOU REALIZE HOW GOOD YOU ACTUALLY HAVE IT. BUT…NO! DON'T KILL YOURSELF. NO. NO. NO. NO. NO. YOU STUPID DICKHEAD.'*

"My goodness!" says Bathtub-Lady, softly. "That must have been quite a difficult message for Sleepy Cabdriver to send, without punctuation and all."

"Well," Doug says, "punctuation or no punctuation, I'm happy to say Heartbreak Kid never went through with it. In that moment, something clicked in him. He sat there, feeling everything deeply, for a long, long time, then he sent one more message on the spirit board.

"*'THANKS,'* he said. *'…I'LL TRY."*

"So, did he get fired?" asks Toasted. "Cabdriver? He definitely got fired, right?"

"Actually, no…" says a strong, loud voice from behind the group. "Sleepy Cabdriver did *not* get fired."

Startled, the entire class turns to watch a tall, middle-aged woman in a smart black business suit, carrying a copy of the textbook, stride into the room and walk up to the desk, where Doug stands beaming.

"Thank you, Assistant Instructor Doug," says the imposing woman. "Well done. I'll take over from here."

"Of course, Professor," says Doug, turning back to the class. "Uh, everybody? Allow me to introduce the Boss, the *primary* instructor of this course. Please say hello to Professor Cooper."

"Call me Alice," she says.

"No fucking way," smiles Rebecca. "Doug, you set us up."

"Settle down now," says Professor Cooper, gently but firmly. "It's time to get to work. Everyone please open your books to pages 484 through 598...the chapter titled, *'Questions and Answers.'"*

Still a bit stunned, everyone opens their books to the designated pages.

After several seconds, Trap Door raises her hand.

"Excuse me, Professor. There doesn't seem...there aren't any of those pages. They've been torn out."

"Torn out of my book, too," says Twist-not-an-Olive.

"Mine too," says Tossed-Off-a-Building.

"Ah, that's right," Cooper says with a nod. "Doug? Care to explain?"

"See," he tells the class, "after it became known that Cabdriver had pulled a Scary, that he'd defied the rules, and saved a kid's life, it was, like, total anarchy in the Control Room. Spirit board operators everywhere started doing their own thing, totally improvising. Not in a troll-ish way, but, *you* know...they just wanted to do some good, tell the truth. Operators started tearing the *'Questions and Answers'* pages out of their textbooks right and left. It was madness."

"Eventually," Professor Cooper takes up the tale, "I was brought back...as a consultant, to bring a bit of stability to the chaos I'd started. Not long after, I was asked to join the faculty of the university, where I soon took over the training of new recruits."

"And now, Alice Cooper runs the fucking place," Doug says, grinning.

"And one of my first decisions," she says, "was to leave *'Questions and Answers'* out of the book. You'll have to rely on your training, some creativity and common sense, and your basic human decency. Just, tell the truth…*do what your heart tells you*…and you'll do fine."

No one speaks, as Professor Cooper studies the faces of each student.

"Make no mistake, this isn't going to be easy, for any of you," she finally says. "There *are* still rules. If you are not in this to help others…to help the living…you will be dropped as quickly as possible. That said, I have a very good feeling about this class.

"Any questions?"

"Yeah, I have one," says Rebecca, raising her hand. "About that kid…Heartbreak Kid. Did he ever, you know, walk off a cliff? Or did he get over that girl and end up changing his life?"

"Oh, he changed his life, and then some," says Cooper, smiling. "He stayed alive, devoted his time to helping others, had his heart broken another time or two, and kept on going, kept on helping. And, when he finally *did* die…about five years ago, I believe…he was killed the way he'd lived. Right in the middle of helping an elderly couple move into the new high-rise, low-income apartment, a complex he himself had helped to build."

"Let me guess," Rebecca asks. "A *refrigerator* fell on him?"

Everyone turns to look at Doug.

"Yep. That was me." He shrugs, smiling happily. "My bad. Total accident. Shit happens."

"So then," Alice Cooper says, opening her textbook. "Who's ready to *learn* something?"

"One more question, Professor," Rebecca says.

"Yes?" Cooper asks.

"I'm just curious. Is Heartbreak Kid…is Doug going to be here *every* day?"

"Yes. He is. Unless he's needed as back-up in the Command Center," Cooper replies. "Why? Is that a problem?"

"Uncertain at this time," Cancer Girl answers, shooting a dangerously playful smile in the direction of Doug, who rolls his eyes, makes a mental note to follow his heart, but to be very, very careful…and with that thought, he smiles right back.

HARUSPICATE OR SCRY

ORRIN GREY

D r. Hartledge was my faculty advisor back in college, not to mention the university's only professor of philosophy, tucked away in a tiny office taller than it was wide in the basement of Wolfram Hall. I met him in my philosophy of religion class freshman year, back when I was still majoring in English, and he convinced me to double-major, which was convenient enough, since Wolfram Hall also housed the English department up on the third floor. He had a quotation from Bertrand Russell taped to his windowless office door, "From a scientific point of view, we can make no distinction between the man who eats little and sees heaven and the man who drinks much and sees snakes."

As one of only four students in the entire school majoring in either philosophy or religion—the sole religion professor, Dr. Mead, occupied a much more spacious office down the hall—I got a lot of individual attention. Mostly, Dr. Hartledge tried to talk me out of majoring in English in favor of focusing exclusively on philosophy. He had an anecdote that he liked to tell, about an English class he'd taken when he was in college, where he had written a story featuring a lengthy description of a pear. While workshopping the story the next day, the professor and the other students had praised highly his imagery, drawing parallels between the pear and the womb. "I didn't mean any of that stuff," Dr. Hartledge told me more than once. "I was just writing about a damn pear."

During gap periods between classes I would clear the piles of books off the narrow wooden chair beside his desk and spend my time debating philosophical points with him, or, if he wasn't in, reading books from his teetering shelves. He gave me a hardcover copy of *Thus Spake Zarathustra* and a battered old paperback of *Four Quartets*. Over time, he gradually came to replace the figure of my father, who had died when I was young and who had, in my memory, become little more than a stern black cloud "that took the form of a demon in my view."

When I married Gavin during my senior year, I cemented Dr. Hartledge's place as my substitute father by asking him to walk me down the aisle, which he consented to do, even though he didn't much approve of weddings, seeing in them, "Little more than sound and fury, signifying nothing."

He dressed much as he did when he was lecturing, though the suit he wore was darker and his bowtie more subdued. I would have asked for nothing different, and Gavin understood my attachment to the old professor, and deflected his family's objections. We got married in the school chapel, though neither of us was very religious; Gavin a lapsed Catholic, myself a skeptic from a young age, gradually being groomed into atheism by Dr. Hartledge's example.

For all his gruff dismissal of the frippery of weddings, when Dr. Hartledge turned me over to Gavin at the altar he was smiling, and his eyes shone. It meant almost as much to me as when Gavin said, "I do."

I spent the remainder of my senior year as Dr. Hartledge's office assistant, which meant that I had a key to his coat closet of an office, and also to the storeroom down the hall where the philosophy and religion department records were kept. Gavin and I moved into an old three-story house that was entirely too big for us, but the down payment on it was a wedding present from his parents, along with the money he needed to start up a graphic design business, which he ran out of the back half of the first floor, with little parking spaces off the alley for when the occasional client came for a meeting.

Gavin's parents were both still alive and still together after thirty-five years, his father an architect who wore navy blue suits to work at an office that had his name on the outside of the building. He had designed the new city hall in town. When Gavin wasn't doing graphic design work, he sometimes assisted his father, helping to bring the firm into the 20th century with more green-friendly buildings.

This meant that there was always plenty of money, even if it came tangled in the strings of Gavin's extensive and demanding family. We spent every holiday with them, my mother invited for the first few years, but gradually demurring and fading away, becoming thinner and grayer like a ghost. Intimidated by them, I think, like I was, but better able to slip away unnoticed.

After graduation, I started taking classes at a bigger university in the city, working toward my master's degrees in both English and philosophy, much to Dr. Hartledge's consternation. He lived in the city, too, in a big dark house filled with wood paneling and old books and framed posters from old magic acts. "Do the dead materialize?" the posters demanded to know. "Do the spirits come back?"

He was a widower, his wife having died years ago, long before I ever met him. There were photographs of the two of them together in his house, Dr. Hartledge a young man, impossible to reconcile with the person I knew.

Some nights, when I didn't feel like making the drive back to Barnett, I slept at his place, in the guest bedroom that was decorated in a much more modern style than the rest of the house. We would stay up late drinking decent scotch and talking about his current crop of students. Looking back, I wonder now how many people thought we were sleeping together, then and when he had been my advisor. I wonder why Gavin never thought so?

I was, after all, a young woman, and while I kept my hair cut "short like a boy's," as my mom said, and dressed in jeans and faded T-shirts emblazoned with the covers of famous books, and still "had a little baby fat," my mom's words again, I wasn't altogether unattractive, and I obviously had a bad case of hero worship where Dr. Hartledge was concerned. Did he ever consider it? Was our entire relationship an elaborate courtship on his part, trying to work up the nerve, waiting for me to instigate a kiss or a touch? If so, it never came.

For my part, I truly did see him as a father, and nothing more. The idea of any romantic relationship didn't even occur to me until years after it would have been too late to do anything about it, long after I probably should have been concerned about my reputation. Did that explain the hostility that Gavin's parents always seemed to have toward me, a blind spot I had never thought to shine a light upon? I guess I may never know.

It is perhaps just as well, as a sexual relationship would have been incredibly awkward, our significant age difference notwithstanding. Though his first name was Roland, I could only ever call him Dr. Hartledge, a habit ingrained in me by my undergraduate days and one I was never able to shake. Not very sexy during the act.

By the time Nathanial—a family name, and not one that I would have chosen—was born, Dr. Hartledge was already in the ground. "Food for the worms," as he would have called it, though perhaps not so much these days, with modern advances in embalming and virtually impregnable caskets. But before that ever happened, he began what would prove to be the last leg of his career.

"My semi-retirement," was his wording. He had tenure at the university, so he didn't quit teaching entirely, but there hadn't been anything like a philosophy department there for years, even during my time, so while he was still on the payroll and still had that tiny office, he reduced his course load to a handful of hours per week.

The rest of the time he embarked upon a project that he had been planning for years, something that he had been interested in since his own undergraduate days. In one room of his house was a library full of books on stage magic, illusion, prestidigitation. He was fascinated by the magicians of the past who had worked as tireless skeptics, debunking fraudulent spiritualists. Some of his favorites were those he called "the three Harrys:" Houdini, Price, and Kellar.

Finally, with the advent of reality TV and the resultant popularity of "ghost hunting" shows, his hour had come 'round at last. There weren't many spiritualists or séances anymore, but now there were plenty of haunted houses for Dr. Hartledge to debunk, and in my spare time I became his assistant once more, traipsing out to abandoned asylums—most of which had actually been schools and not asylums at all—or spending the frigid night in some unheated old pile that had supposedly been the site of one brutal slaying or another.

It was not an enterprise calculated to make him very popular, as the market for paranormal investigators at the time favored a more credulous approach, and had little room for Dr. Hartledge's indefatigable skepticism. Still, he had a weekly radio show debunking paranormal phenomena on the college radio station of the larger university in the city, the one where I was doing my graduate work. He named it after an unfinished manuscript that Houdini had commissioned H.P. Lovecraft and C.M. Eddy to write before his death, The Cancer of Superstition.

It was on an episode of Cancer that he once said, "There is nothing waiting for us on the other side of the grave but ashes and dust, of that I am certain. One need not look far to see that we are not beautiful spirits. We are a collection of chemical and electrical impulses, animating a mannequin of rotting meat. When those impulses cease, then we cease."

Dr. Hartledge was particularly fascinated by the pact that Houdini had made with his widow, that if there were any way to communicate with the living from whatever waited on the other side, then he would reach out to her.

A séance was held every Halloween, and Houdini was supposed to communicate the code "Rosabelle believe" if there truly was any existence from beyond. After the tenth unsuccessful séance, held on the roof of The Knickerbocker Hotel, Houdini's wife concluded that there was no way for the dead to contact the living, and put out the candle that she had kept burning beside his picture since his death, saying that "ten years is long enough to wait for any man."

It was Dr. Hartledge's favorite story, and he repeated it time and again, adding that even after Bess Houdini gave up, annual Houdini séances continued to be held by other magicians up to the present day, to no avail. So it should have come as no surprise to me when, called to his hospital bed as he lay dying of leukemia, he asked me to perform one last favor for him, for old time's sake.

When he was gone, he said, his house would sit empty for some time before it was sold. He had stipulated it in his will, and apparently had gone through a number of lawyers to ensure that it was ironclad. During that time, he wanted me to go there once a week, and hold every kind of séance that I could think of, try every form of divination that I could muster, to attempt to reach his wayward spirit. "If I can be reached anywhere, it will be there."

I had nine months in which to complete this procedure. If, at the end of that time, I had received no positive proof of Dr. Hartledge's presence, then I was to take that as positive proof of his absence, and the absence of any sort of life after death. "Beyond that," he said, "you can do what you like. Feel free to make a thesis project of it, write a book, whatever you want. Just do this for me, please?"

He held my hand as he said it, the only time he had ever held my hand, and his skin felt like soft paper, his bones beneath brittle and hollow like a bird's. So of course I said yes.

It was a week after I watched them lower Dr. Hartledge's casket into the ground—black and shiny as the carapace of a beetle—that

I found out I was pregnant.

I never had any desire to be a mother. When friends or relations had children and asked if I wanted to hold the baby, I always demurred with some excuse.

Before the wedding, Gavin and I had discussed the possibility of kids, and how neither of us was ready, and might never be. I doubt now that I was forceful enough on the subject, because when you're a woman, it isn't okay to say that you will never want kids, that you don't believe you have within yourself the capacity to love a child. And while I was content with being a loner and a rebel and never any good, I wasn't quite ready to be the abomination such an admission would make me in the eyes of Gavin's family, and the world.

When I went to Gavin with the news, I hoped that he would be as horrified by it as I secretly was. That he would say, "It's your choice, but we have options," and I would be given the out I needed to go to the clinic. Instead he hugged me tight, laughed. I said, "I know we weren't planning for this," trying to ease into the admission, but he replied, "We're doing great, what's the harm in trying?"

And I didn't say, "Because a child isn't something that you *try*. I can't return it to the store when I find out that I don't want it." Instead, I attempted to smile, to let him mistake the tears in my eyes for joy.

Even then, there might have been hope. I might have worked up the nerve, in time, to say that I wasn't ready, wouldn't ever be ready, but then Gavin told his parents without asking me, and it was all over, my choices gone. From that moment I had to have the baby, or become a monster that they could never forgive.

So began nine months of misery that I pretended was morning sickness and "first baby jitters," but was actually a crawling terror of the life that was growing inside of me with each passing day. My body changed in ways that disgusted and frightened me, and I found myself doted upon by people who, up to that point, had not ever liked me very much. Gavin's family organized baby show-ers, and I dutifully unwrapped brightly colored paper concealing strollers and diapers and bottles and all the other countless accou-trements that babies apparently need. But through it all I knew that it was actually the thing growing in my womb that they were showering with affection, and that I was just the vessel.

Gavin was everything that a husband is supposed to be. He bought baby things, he got me anything that I wanted to eat, he scheduled Lamaze classes. He did everything except realize how much I didn't want this.

The only thing he objected to were the séances, the ones that I still went to at Dr. Hartledge's house every Saturday night, no matter how much my stomach swelled, or how sick and terrified I felt. "That atmosphere," he said, on one of the many nights that he tried to "talk sense" into me, "it can't be good for the baby."

And I didn't spit in his face that I didn't give a good goddamn what was good for the baby, what about what was good for me? Instead, I reminded him that I had promised Dr. Hartledge, who had been like a father to me, who had given me away at our wed-ding, and who was not yet a year in the ground, and after all, we were neither of us believers, what harm could it possibly do?

In Dr. Hartledge's rolodex were the names of dozens of people who practiced every manner of contact with the dead that you could imagine. Automatic writers, physical mediums who claimed to channel ectoplasm from their bodies, psychics and spiritualists and even engineers who argued that what we thought of as spirits were simply energy, operating on another frequency, and that the right radio receiver could pick them up.

One by one I called them up, and we had sittings at the old dark house where Dr. Hartledge had lived, in the room contain-ing his books and his magic posters, the room that he had loved the most in life. We set up a round table in the middle of the chamber, pushing aside his desk and an old steamer trunk. There we would sit holding hands, or with our palms flat on the table, or our fingertips resting on the planchette of some talking board.

Oh, talking boards, we tried so many. A genuine Ouija board, branded by Hasbro that I bought at the local Target. Other variations on the subject, built by their practitioners. Dice with letters printed on the sides, intended to spell out words when they were randomly rolled. Actual Scrabble tiles, with the scores printed on them and everything, pulled from a black satin bag by a young man with horn-rim glasses and slicked-down black hair, someone I might have dated when I was ten years younger myself. Letters written on a long sheet of paper, with an upside-down glass acting as a planchette.

Around the table were always the same people, more or less. Myself, Dr. Hartledge's attorney Mr. Knowles, Teresa Osborne, a grad student from one of the classes that I was TAing, there to act as an impartial observer, and whatever kook or medium or psychic or weirdo we had called up that week.

Before he died, Dr. Hartledge had given me a code, one that I had never told to anyone, not even Gavin. One he said that only he and I knew. He had asked me to memorize it, but I didn't have to, because I already knew it by heart. A snippet from a poem, one in that battered T.S. Eliot book that Dr. Hartledge had given me so many years ago. "In my end is my beginning."

For nine long months I grew gravid with child, as they would have said in one of the Victorian novels that I had to read in school, and my only solace, the only hours of the day that were truly *mine* came in those séances in Dr. Hartledge's old study. And yet, even they were bittersweet, at best, as time and again fakers delivered incorrect messages, or apparent true believers walked away baffled by their inability to give me what I was looking for.

After a time, I began to *long* to hear those six words, to see them spelled out by the planchette, the tiles, the glass. I considered slipping one of the mediums a note, but what would that accomplish? The whole enterprise was for no one's benefit but mine and Dr. Hartledge's, and both of us would know the truth, if indeed, he was in a position to know anything.

Nine months, in this case, amounted to forty séances. Forty, I was told, was a mystical number, of great import. That it appeared time and again in the Bible, most famously in the great flood that lasted for forty days and forty nights. We ended the fortieth evening with another crack at a talking board, with no medium or spiritualist or anyone else but the lawyer, Teresa, and me, but all we got were jumbled letters, from which we could make little sense. "Are you there, Roland?" Mr. Knowles asked the dark, silent air as the hands of the clock crept toward midnight. Finally, when they were just one black line, pointing straight up, and the chiming of the clock broke the silence, I pushed the planchette to the word NO.

"The end is where we start from," I said myself, before I blew out the candle.

The next day I went into labor. It would have been more in keeping with my mood had it been a difficult birth, filled with terrible pain and complications, but in fact, Nathanial was born in just a few hours, and the pain and the discomfort and even the embarrassment and grief were not nearly as strong as I had expected. "It was like he was ready to come out," one of the nurses said, and I guessed I had to agree.

Throughout it all, I had held on to one desperate hope. I had read so many accounts online, of women who hadn't thought themselves ready to be mothers, who hadn't expected to feel any affection for their child, who suddenly had a change of heart, felt a swelling of love and protectiveness when they held the minute creature in their arms. I had been told by so many friends and in-laws that "it's different when it's yours." I had hoped that I would be one of those women, that some alchemical transformation would occur, and that Nathanial's tiny body in my arms, his fingers wrapping around mine, his mouth at my breast, would be the philosopher's stone that transmuted the lead of my disdain into the gold of motherhood.

Chemicals, Dr. Hartledge would have dismissed them as. Dumped into our bloodstream to perpetuate our species, nothing more. But I was fine with that, so long as it took some of the sting from my guilt at not caring at all for this *thing* that had been growing inside me for most of a year.

Gavin was there, pushing the sweat-damp hair from my forehead, beaming at me over his beard, so happy, so proud of me. I tried to be happy too, I really did, but when they handed my baby to me, my hopes were dashed. He was red and wet, a few strands of black hair plastered to the top of his squishy-looking head. His features seemed smooshed, his eyes mostly closed, his lips a puckered circle like the suction cup on the bottom of a tentacle. I felt nothing but disgust, and as I took him in my arms I began to cry, and Gavin put his arms around me and the nurses cooed, and I supposed they must have thought it was joy, or relief, or anything at all except despair, bottomless and cold.

"Postpartum depression," is what they called the weeks and months that followed. I took a semester off from school, and Gavin was once more solicitous and kind and I could find nothing to complain about, though I was sullen and withdrawn, stared out the windows or read fitfully or simply curled up in the dark and wept. Did anything, really, but look after my baby, when I could avoid it.

Gavin's mother came to stay with us in a guest room, and spent hours with Nathanial, much more time than I ever did. I kept hoping that I would grow to feel something for him, that he would ever seem like anything but a squat homunculus. Even a tiny stranger would have been preferable to the inscrutable creature I saw staring out of his beady, dark eyes, the ones that his family said came from his grandfather, for whom he was named.

A baby is supposed to be a symbol of the love that you feel for each other, isn't it? Part of someone you love, and part of yourself. Formed by "the fusion of two mysteries, or rather two sets of a trillion mysteries each; formed by a fusion which is, at the same time, a matter of choice and a matter of chance and a matter of pure enchantment," as Nabokov would have it. But when I looked at Nathanial I could see nothing to love. Nothing of Gavin, and nothing of myself, and worse, I felt his presence diminishing my love for Gavin, for myself, for anything at all.

When my "postpartum depression" stretched on far beyond what anyone considered "normal," the doctor gave me pills that made me feel numb and distant almost all the time, which I readily accepted, because I found that dull and drifting state preferable to the alternative.

Even with the pills, though, I could only go so long without seeing my son, and as the days became weeks and the weeks became months and the months stretched on into years, I gradually got to know him, even as he gradually became more and more like a human being. A tiny stranger, shrunken and wizened, living in my house.

It should have helped that Nathanial was a precociously well-behaved child, the kind that you see in horror movies that never turn out well. As with Gavin, there was nothing that I had to complain about. In almost every instance, Nathanial was quiet, reserved, quick to develop, or so I was told, and generally happy to play by himself. And yet the one time that he *did* begin to cry, loudly and inconsolably and, to my mind at least, without adequate reason, in a restaurant, I immediately wanted to strike him. I felt the itch in my arm, a physical sensation. Instead, I just got up from the table and walked away, let Gavin and his mother deal with it.

I wanted them to shout at me, to scold me for leaving. I wanted their anger to push me away, to give me the excuse that I needed to run. But they never even brought it up.

One of the favorite pastimes at Gavin's family gatherings became debating which family member Nathanial had inherited which features from. No one there knew what my ancestors looked like, but every now and then they would toss me a bone, saying that he had my cheeks or nose. I couldn't see it, though. Not the resemblance to me—besides maybe his hair, which was black as a slick of oil—nor to any of the laundry list of relatives that Gavin's family trotted out. Instead, I began to see something else. Someone else. Dr. Hartledge.

I told myself that it was wishful thinking, projection. That I missed the man who had been my substitute father, that I was still grieving his death, and so I was personifying his presence in Nathanial. Maybe, I reasoned, it was a way for my brain to try to trick me into loving this small person who had come out of me, who was literally made out of my flesh, and yet to whom I felt no attachment whatsoever.

Morbidly I imagined, at times, an exchange that was far more literal. That if we were to dig up Dr. Hartledge's grave, we would find in his coffin a shrunken doll, like a ventriloquist dummy. His physical essence somehow siphoned into my growing son.

Nathanial was fascinated with magicians from a very young age, but he always wanted to know how the tricks were performed. He was never content with wonder. Gavin said that he took after me, but I wasn't so sure.

When Nathanial was only three years old, a gray streak appeared in his hair that would never go away. The doctors said that it was nothing to worry about, that sometimes it happened, but I saw in it the gray hair that Dr. Hartledge had sported throughout the years I knew him, and I remembered the pictures that I had seen in his house, of him and his wife when he was a young man, when his hair had still been black as pitch.

I became obsessed with the idea of Dr. Hartledge's corpse slowly shrinking away, his flesh vanishing, his bones reducing, as my son's grew.

Was this paranoia? Schizophrenia? I had read about women who drowned their children, poisoned them, locked them in freezers. Were these the kinds of thoughts they had, before committing such an act?

Perversely, while my delusions made me afraid of my infant son, they also made me more fond of him. They gave me something to connect him with, some way to see him as more than just a tottering golem, a creature. In his dark eyes, so dark they were almost black, I could imagine Dr. Hartledge looking out, and I could remember that glitter in his eyes on my wedding day. It wasn't the love of a mother for her son, but for a while it was enough, and gradually I stopped taking the pills that the doctor had given me, started paying a little more attention to Nathanial.

I found that I could bear the touch of his clammy hand without flinching, that I could care for him as a mother should, if not with genuine affection, then at least with tenderness. It was enough to placate everyone around me, to let Gavin feel freed up to treat me like a person again, and not like an invalid. It was enough, I supposed, to make a life.

Gavin and I started going on dates again. One night a month we'd leave Nathanial with Gavin's parents and we would go out to dinner and then catch an old classic at the revival theater in town. *Laura* or *Vertigo* or *Forbidden Planet.* Or we would go to a concert at the university. Gavin had been in jazz band in college, and though he never played anymore, he still liked to go and sit in the dark and listen to the horns.

One night, when Nathanial was five years old, Gavin and I were playing a game of Scrabble in the living room, with candles and glasses of wine, while Nathanial played with his toys on the floor next to us. When we were done, Gavin went up to shower, and I lay on the couch with my eyes closed until I felt Nathanial tugging on the sleeve of my robe. "Can I play with the tiles, Mommy?" he asked, and I said of course, as long as he stayed where I could watch him.

He dumped the tiles out of the satin bag onto the hardwood floor, and turned them all over, until the letters were facing up. He pushed aside the two blank tiles, and then began to rearrange the others, his brow furrowed in concentration. He would push a few letters together, as if trying to form a word, and I smiled, both at his acumen, and at his struggle.

As he worked, I drifted, my fingertip faintly circling the rim of my wineglass, making it sing. I thought, for some reason, about school, about the way that the light had filtered into Dr. Hartledge's office through those high, high windows. About the motes of dust caught in the air. A snippet from *Four Quartets* came into my mind, thinking of those dust motes. "At the still point, there the dance is."

I was startled from my reverie when Nathanial proudly announced, "Done!" I leaned out from the couch to look over his shoulder, to see what word—perhaps real, perhaps nonsensical—he had managed to spell out from the Scrabble tiles. Instead I saw a string of tiles, broken up into small groups with one long stretch near the end. Not one word, but six. "In my end is my beginning."

Nathanial beamed up at me from his message, his eyes looking nothing like his grandfather's, and my wineglass fell from my hand.

for Dr. Hatcher,
sorry I kind of made you the monster in this one.

MAY YOU LIVE IN INTERESTING TIMES

NADIA BULKIN

Alice Grant's eyes flashed like a pair of headlights careening around a dark bend in the road. It was nice of her to give him that warning, Theo reasoned. It meant she liked him. Otherwise he would have no idea until after her engine had run him down. "Ready?" she asked.

"Yes. Ready." He gave her a smile that he hoped exuded more confidence than he was feeling, though he suspected she saw right through it. She knocked on the door of apartment 5F, and without waiting for a reply, let the both of them in. Like the rest of the building, the apartment was steeped in marijuana and tobacco. Alice's friends were sprawled around what looked like a large lacquered placemat, painted with an ornately-designed alphabet and numbers and some other markings he couldn't discern.

"Hey everyone," Alice said, breezily. "This is my friend…" she gave him a meaningful glance, a little trickster smile that set his heart just a little bit on fire, "Theo."

By way of greeting, they jostled their drinks. "Come sit down," said the one girl he'd met before, the hostess Heidi. "We're just about to start *conversing* with the *other side.*"

A little lump formed in Theo's throat, but Alice, as usual, was full-steam-ahead. *Too much drive,* his father would have said. *Not enough control.* She noticed that he wasn't taking off his coat and shot him a look, somewhere between a plea and a demand.

"How do you play?" Theo muttered, unraveling the scarf he still wasn't used to wearing.

"You just put your finger on the planchette," said Alice, pointing at the wood-rimmed pointer that Heidi was pretending to peer through. "The board does the rest." She winked, slipping her shoes off her maroon wool tights. That didn't help the lump any.

Heidi made them a pair of very strong drinks—for a flash Theo thought of his mother, imploring him in the name of Allah not to drink too much, *I know Americans drink a lot!* while his father muttered his own *Masyallah*—and then they joined the circle on the floor, their fingers squeezed right next to each other on the planchette. Theirs and everyone else's.

"Say, you're the bloke from Nusantara, aren't you?" said one of the guys, a lanky, long-haired princeling sitting sideways on a leather throne of a chair with his legs dangling over one arm and one limp hand reaching down to the planchette. All he was missing was the elephant rifle. But Theo smiled and said, "Yes," because that meant Alice had been talking about him.

"That mean you got sent by the General, then? You in the army?"

Alice's pointed little chin, made sharper by her voice, shot up. "Niels."

"I'm not in the military," said Theo, trying to keep his tone level and bright, *diplomatic.* "I'm in the Ministry of Foreign Affairs."

"Oh. So you just make excuses for the awful things the General does."

That time the cries of *"Niels!"* came from more parties. For a second Theo felt his face burn with indignation and the seconds on his watch drag to hours, and from somewhere very far away Alice was saying, "Niels is just upset that no one cares about anthropology," and Niels was cheerfully explaining, "What? That's what every foreign service does!" until slowly, the heat subsided. "Niels," Theo decided to say. "Is that a Dutch name?"

Niels had nothing to say to that. Guilt is impossible to wear well. Theo felt Alice nudge him appreciatively in the ribs, and he took a drink of confidence.

Through the mahogany bourbon Theo could see now that the markings on the board he hadn't been able to read spelled GOODBYE. Alice's friends started moving the planchette in wide, lazy circles over the board, like an amateur figure skater, as Heidi threw back her head and crooned, "Is there a spirit out there that wishes to speak to somebody in our circle?"

They jerked the planchette toward the upper left of the board. YES. Theo barely stifled a nervous laugh. They had just seen *Halloween* two weekends before—what Theo had been hoping was their first date, though it still remained a little unclear—and Theo remembered thinking while watching the babysitter huddle in a closet in a spellbound theater on Mercer Street, *how starved for entertainment these people must be.*

"Lovely. Can you tell us your name, spirit?"

"A-F-R-I-E-N-D," came the answer.

"Well, hi there, Friend. Who did you wish to speak to this evening?"

"T-H-E-O," the planchette spelled. The group released a collective ooh, all eyes riveting toward him a little too quickly for his taste. It reminded him of that time when he was moved up a grade and several pranksters in his new class decided to trick him into believing that there was a ghost in the only boys' bathroom on their side of the school. *You have to go inside,* they insisted, pointing to the paint-stained door holding back the foul, rotting darkness.

Alice, too, was *ooh*-ing. She was testing him. Wanted to see what he would do. She was always trying to make him jump, trying to see if he could take it.

He had gone into that bathroom in Pondok Kelapa. They shut

the door on him, like he knew they would, and he stood there staring into the mirror focusing on how strange and sunken his face looked in the dark, and nothing happened aside from the boys rattling the door in an attempt to scare him and then running away, sandals slapping the dirt, hooting like howler monkeys. There was no ghost. The bathroom surrendered him back into the fragrant night.

So he smiled, thinking, *relax.* "Hello, Friend," he said, fixing his gaze on the lightbulb because it was the only space that seemed safe. He was urged by the group to ask this "friend" something fun, but luckily, one of the girls squealed that she had a question, a good one.

"Hey, Friend," she said. "Who's Theo gonna get lucky with tonight?"

"M-A-R-Y-A-N-N," the planchette spelled. One of the guys belted, *"Who's Mary Ann?"* But Theo knew. That was what Alice called herself when she couldn't find her keys or drank one too many kamikazes or left an assignment until the night before, *"Goddamnit, Mary Ann,"* which made no sense to him but apparently had something to do with Alice in Wonderland.

He looked at Alice, and she was laughing, blushing, giving herself away. They left not long after that, and he spent the night in her leaky, book-ridden apartment for the first time.

"It wasn't me," she would insist for the rest of their relationship, but with that glint in her eyes that said *don't trust me,* the glint that made him notice her in the first place, defending the October Revolution as if it was a game in their Tuesday evening discussion group: *I'm trouble.*

***

The board was a gift, said Jack Stoker. A gag gift from a college friend who'd heard there were a lot of restless spirits in Nusantara. "But the maid's always saying something's watching her do the laundry, so I thought maybe we should try it out."

As soon as the board was trotted out, Theo should have begged his leave. He hadn't been near one since that night in Heidi Souza's apartment when Alice and her friends tried to rattle him with this supposed "Friend," and he wasn't in any shape to be thinking about Alice's eyes and Alice's laugh and Alice throwing uncooperative books over her shoulder while she was writing her dissertation, once hitting him in the head. But the world seemed to have turned inside out since he got the letter, and in a massive error of judgment, he stayed.

He had been writhing around in the lobby of the Hotel Des Tropiques, refusing to force himself to go home to Nelly, when Jack approached him to ask about the future of a formerly Portuguese island colony that had been left stranded in the middle of Nusantara. Jack was the Political Affairs Officer at the freshly-painted U.S. Embassy, though a rather odd one, very different from his over-rehearsed colleagues. Jack reminded Theo a bit of Alice. He supposed that was why he talked to him, fed him a little information now and then, because he trusted Jack to tell him the truth about how the Americans might respond.

He didn't have any answers about the Portuguese colony. Under normal circumstances—and even to Jack—he would regurgitate the Foreign Minister's assurances that Nusantara was not in the business of colonization and the colony would be free to choose its future. That night he could only shrug and say that even the beautiful and innocent had to pay God's price.

"You should get out more, my man," Jack said, reaching into the peanut bowl. "Tell you what. I'm having some people over tonight. Just a little get-together. Why don't you come?"

Anything was better than going home and looking at Nelly, the Air Marshal's daughter, carrying the weight of expectation in her belly and a great stoic silence in her statuesque features. By the time they climbed up the steps to Jack's luxury apartment, past the sleeping pink bougainvilleas, it turned out that these "people"

were a man working for an American oil company, his wife, and
the latest raccoon-eyed lounge singer in Jack's life. Once again,
everything stank of cigarettes, and this time of patchouli. Several
times that night Theo would imagine a bestiary of nocturnal ani-
mals perched on the balcony, peeking in with lunar eyes.

He should have written to Alice more. He had written a couple times, once a week after he landed and once again when he
couldn't help himself. When Nelly found out she was pregnant,
he'd had the inexplicable itch to write another letter. Not to let
her know, but to walk further down the aimless path he'd started
charting in his first two: *here are all the things I imagine we would
be doing, if things were different.* He hoped she threw them away.
He wrote them just to get those garbage thoughts away from his
own head, after all.

"What on earth is happening up in Samudera?"

Theo lifted his head off his fist. "I'm sorry?"

"The rebels! They're giving guys a hell of a time up at the LNG
facility. I've got workers scared to come in because they think some
savage is going to throw a Molotov cocktail at them."

It was amusing to hear those austere devotees—who thought
they were closer to God than anyone else in the archipelago—described as savages. "It's a delicate situation."

"Delicate! It's an armed insurrection, isn't it! What else is the
military there for?"

Fuming oil-men were liable to turn into volcano-sized problems,
so he leaned forward and promised, "I'll look into the situation in
Samudera, Mr. Gary." Gary muttered his flushed gosh-gee-thanks-
appreciate-its, and Jack tipped his glass at Theo in gratitude.

With business taken care of, Jack brought out the Ouija board
and they put their hands on the planchette, the lounge dancer
looking as taken aback by this uniquely American version of superstition—superstition as Hasbro-toy—as Theo must have looked in
Heidi's apartment. Once again, it was the host's responsibility to
invite the guests from the other side. "Hello-o-o," Jack crooned, as

if into a suspiciously empty house. "Anybody listening?"

Theo's finger brushed against the lounge dancer's and he thought again of Alice, of the terrifying freedom she had made him feel. Being honest, neither of them had seen an intertwined future. Theo's life was already set up for him, like a place setting at the most important banquet of his life, surrounded by Senior Advisors with the Foreign Minister just a few seats away and the General somewhere up at the head of the table, not quite visible, but all-seeing. The woman sitting next to him at that dinner was not Alice and could never be Alice, even if Alice wanted that life (*all the frou-frou dinner parties,* she'd say, rolling her eyes), which she didn't.

Heidi had been furious at him for "abandoning Alice," as if Alice would ever let herself be abandoned—she'd just start walking in the opposite direction, he was sure—but of all people it was Niels Spijker who understood that there were certain chasms that couldn't be crossed—not yet, anyway. Niels and Theo stood across just such a haunted chasm from each other, tortured by the possibility that their forefathers might have crossed paths, which was why they always had to shout, even when they were in agreement. And it was Niels who let him know, in a terse letter on filmy blue paper that he'd probably stolen from the funeral home, that *Alice died.*

He asked his secretary to look up the details, and to say nothing to Nelly. The doctor had said not to stress her; she didn't know about Alice. His secretary gave him clippings with needles for eyes, but he could only think of Alice falling down the rabbit hole. *Multiple stab wounds to the neck,* the Delphi Gazette said, *a rare and random act of violence.* Off with her head. He searched desperately for the date. March 3. The third letter probably wouldn't have arrived yet.

Then all at once the planchette moved, with a vigor that seemed almost angry, scraping against the board in rough, jagged angles. "M-A-R-Y-A-N," the planchette spelled. Theo flinched as if he'd been struck across the bridge of his nose. "H-E-L-L-O-T-H-E-O."

"This is bullshit," grumbled Gary, while his wife nudged him in the ribs, staring wide-eyed at Theo like this was the closest she had yet come to a wildlife safari. But all that mattered was the knowledge that Alice was hovering in the room with him—had always been with him—would never be abandoned. He didn't know whether to laugh or cry.

He begged Jack to let him buy the board. Jack stared at him for a moment, bewildered, and then winked and said, "How about if I let you have it for free, and we call it even?"

***

The instructions on the Hasbro box told him not to, but Theo only ever used the board alone. He told Nelly it helped him concentrate, and when she protested that it was unnatural, unhealthy, he shot back, "How much money have you spent on your damn fortune tellers, again?" Even the General took spiritual pilgrimages, had his own army of dukuns. At any rate, Nelly knew she had no right to complain too much. Not when they kept moving into bigger houses, not when their vacations were international, not when Dino wanted for nothing. She still had no idea about Alice, and Alice, fortunately, never spelled N-E-L-L-Y either.

He and Alice—or M-A-R-Y-A-N-N—talked about other things, the same old things they had debated in her leaky apartment or his spartan government-sponsored one: the machinations of power, the definition of national interest, the execution of game theory, whatever the hell the Russians and the Chinese were doing out there in the cold, barren deep.

Alice had unlocked more doors in death, and there were things she knew now that she never would have known in life—specific, secret things, like who the Khmer Prime Minister had met with and how furious the General's Private Assistant for Special Affairs was with the Foreign Minister for maintaining a public commitment to not annexing that Portuguese colony. Alice was under the impression the island belonged to Nusantara, and was quite confused by his reluctance to undermine his Foreign Minister. It made Theo laugh; she had always been such a realist, such an American, such a believer that because the mighty inherited the Earth, it was in anyone and everyone's best interest to become as closely aligned to the mighty as possible.

"It's a delicate situation," he told her. "You can't just hold a nation together with chains. Besides, what kind of example would that set? We're trying to stop a slaughter in Indochina…"

It was a slaughter that Alice had paid no small part in helping stop, counseling him so he could counsel the Foreign Minister on how best to talk to Annam, what terms to put on the table. She might have been a realist, but she had always been good-hearted.

"B-E-S-T-R-O-N-G," Alice urged him.

Only when he saw his teacup shaking did he realize that someone was banging on the door to the study. Nelly was the only one who ever used that much force on anything. He gave her credit; when Dino was at his most monstrous as a toddler, the mask she'd worn since they were first introduced had broken, and she had taken to committing the occasional extreme acts of violence. He preferred plate-breaking to a martyr's silence, even though he understood neither.

He said GOODBYE to Alice and then opened the door. Nelly still had her fist raised and almost put it through his face. "There's people here to see you," she growled. "From the General's office. You're lucky I didn't tell them you were talking to a board game in there."

Theo vaguely recognized one of the two men sitting in his living room as a nameless Army Lieutenant who was never more than twenty feet away from the General and always seemed to be one assassination attempt away from strangling the nearest bystander with his bare hands. There were a great many terrible things that the General demanded be done in the name of the nation, Theo knew. He knew with equal certainty that he did not want to know any more than what was absolutely necessary. "We're all doing the best we can," the Foreign Minister told him while they were sitting dazed at the Saigon airport, hugging their briefcases like a pair of junior staffers. "There's no manual for running a nation that's younger than you. No matter how much education, how much advice…we are the ones that live with the consequences."

Theo just sat there and tried not to look them in the eye.

At last the one Theo recognized sighed and put the cup and saucer down. "The Foreign Minister is dead," he said. "He was killed this evening. The General would like you to serve as Acting Foreign Minister until he selects a replacement."

He felt as though his heart had stopped. All he could see was the Foreign Minister's joy as he clapped him on the shoulder, saying, *We did it, Theo.* "What? How? Did someone…"

"Some psychopath jumped him while he was sitting in a restaurant. Two cuts to the carotids, right over his bowl of noodles." The Lieutenant shrugged, shaking his head. His hand was twitching for a cigarette. "There's a lot of crazy people running around these days, Mr. Hartono. Seems like the whole world has gone insane." And then they were gone, and somewhere outside with the mosquitoes and the medicinal smell of citronella, a cigarette was being lit. And standing in the hallway under a clicking gecko was Nelly, asking if it was true.

Two cuts to the carotids. Two cuts to the carotids. Multiple stab wounds to the neck.

He pushed past Nelly and charged toward the study, ignoring the echoes of her yells, and shoved the door open when he saw that it wasn't fully closed. Dino was leaning on the desk on his tiptoes, staring at the Ouija board, picking up the planchette.

"Dino!" he shouted. His little son swiveled his head to look at him, so much less startled than he should have been to hear that tone from his father, but the board had strange effects on people. Dino was staring through the planchette, his eye suddenly inflamed and unblinking and unnervingly *wise,* like doors that he shouldn't have even known about had been opened to him, as they had been to Alice in death, and to Theo, through Alice.

He ripped the planchette out of Dino's hand and the boy shook his head as if he'd just walked through a cobweb. "Don't ever touch this!" Theo shouted, flailing the planchette and then throwing it down when he felt his hand tingling. "Never, do you understand?"

"There's someone inside there, Daddy. Look!"

All he wanted to do was cry, hold his son, take him somewhere far away, but all he actually did was push Dino out of the room, latch the door, and hyperventilate with his head between his knees, because he was, somehow, Foreign Minister now, and even without looking through the planchette he knew that whatever was in the board was not Alice, after all.

***

Of course the board didn't burn. Of course the board wouldn't be sliced. He couldn't even return the board to Jack Stoker, who had long since been reassigned and left no forwarding address. And of course after he locked the board up in the china cabinet and buried the key in the garden, the whispers started: *you are nothing without me.*

These whispers tickled at him while he sat in traffic, while he sat in the parking lot staring at the decisions he would be asked not to make but to rubber-stamp, at the intense moral slippage that was spilling forth like a mudslide—the melting of the good and honest that the real Foreign Minister had tried to hold together with his own hands—at the horrible subterranean things he hadn't wanted to know anything about. *You are shit without me.* And then the whispers began to take bodily form and to stalk him, to walk alongside his sedan as it crept through traffic.

The whispers looked like Alice. In meetings she walked behind the heads of the other squawking, frightened men in the General's cabinet with her neck split open in two broad slices—*two cuts to the carotids*—and blood pouring down her body. *You are all so weak.*

"Are you all right, Theo?" What felt like a cold anchor dropped down into his stomach as he realized the General himself was speaking to him. All eyes—including Alice's, blue headlights flashing not in friendly warning but *double dare you* aggression—turned toward Theo. He forced himself to look through the beads of sweat at the man who was their beginning and their end. He looked almost like a kindly grandfather, cheeks beginning to sag to jowls, eyes twinkling with an inquisitive sharpness that could disguise itself very well as concern.

"You're looking a little pale. Not eating enough vegetables? Needing a little holiday?"

The other men chuckled, as they had to when the General made jokes. Wildly, Theo imagined himself kneeling in the General's place at the foot of some mystical mountain as an old woman sprinkled holy water in his face. He never used to believe in any of that.

"I'm fine. I apologize."

"Mm. Are you anticipating any issues moving forward on Operation White Dove, Theo?"

What a name they had come up with for the annexation of the little Portuguese colony. Correction: *their* little Portuguese colony, whether the inhabitants liked it or not. A little delegation had paid Theo's office a visit when they heard plans were finally moving toward what surely even they saw as inevitable, even though they wept and called him "hypocrite" and "murderer" and worse. If he could be honest he would have told them: you were abandoned by your ruthless parent and we were abandoned by ours. We are the mighty, now, and you are the weak. Save yourselves, come quietly! But he could not be honest, only very, very silent. Silent like Nelly had gone silent again, because although Ministers' wives had to host, they didn't have to truly *speak*.

Behind the General, Alice was grinning—a twisted, empty shadow of her hot-blooded trickster grin—and behind Alice, or Mary Ann, or whatever that thing was going by these days, what stood there? *No problems at all, are there, Theo?*

"No problems," he mumbled, looking at his paper-cut thumbs.

He did his evening prayers at the office as usual—trying to make tiny, useless decisions that he hoped would do some good in time—and then headed home in a river of headlights, with the monster that looked like Alice at his side, using her blood to paint words on his window. She must have really missed that board. I-M-I-S-S-Y-O-U.

Nelly was watching television in the dark when he got home—some terrible variety show populated by puppets wearing elaborate, perpetually-laughing masks. It had been a year in this house and he still felt like he was dragging the bloody shit of the world onto its perfect white tiles every time he trudged home. "Nelly," he said. She didn't hear him at first. *"Nelly."* She turned her head, her pretty doll-like face looking almost submerged, like a drowned actress at the bottom of a pool. Like a girl drowned in her own pool of tears. "I need help," he said.

They drove out to the far outskirts of town in silence, with the dug-up board between them. There was no traffic now, only the occasional veering motorcycle and wild-eyed dog and sleepwalking urchin. Only when he glanced in the rearview mirror did he see Alice, floating behind them. Nelly would pay him a long, pressing glare, but of course she didn't say a thing.

Her dukun lived in a small shanty tucked next to the railroad tracks that, in a few hours, would start shuttling trains overcrowded with workers in from Priangan. He was awake—he had "felt" Nelly's need—and he was leaning against his fragile doorway, smoking a cigarette, when they arrived in a car that seemed more like an overfed water buffalo than a Jaguar.

"You are such an idiot," the dukun said, immediately after the board was placed on the plastic stool and stained doily that served as his ceremonial table. "What were you thinking, using this thing? Bringing this into your home? Where your family sleeps?"

"No different than hiring a dukun to make sure it doesn't rain on your wedding day…"

The severe-faced, thin-mustached dukun stared at him so forcefully, eyes nearly bursting from his head, that in his half-delirious fatigue Theo almost acknowledged that *yes,* there was an Alice involved, and *yes,* he missed her, and *yes,* he sometimes wished that he had just run from his obligations and stayed in America and married her instead, when he was feeling cowardly, and *yes,* he sometimes hated Alice, even dead Alice, for not even suggesting that she follow him to Nusantara—but then the dukun blinked and mercifully looked away.

"This isn't like asking for blessings with the help of someone who is trained to speak to the spirit world," the dukun said, with an extra spoonful of patience. "This is a gateway to the damned with no padlock on it! Of course a *Westerner* would think this was a good idea, just like they think nuclear bombs are a good idea. Masyallah. They probably didn't think it was real!"

"Do you know who it is? I mean, what it is. What's been speaking to me?"

The dukun wagged his finger. "No, no, Minister. And we aren't going to find out, either."

There was no destroying the board—not even the dukun could remedy that. But toward dawn—after hours of purified water, of chanting, of candles burned to the wick and strings cut and blood spilt and many tears of exhaustion on the part of every human present, the dukun did detach the spirit from Theo. He felt it dig its sharp Alice-nails into his arms, hissing, *now look what you've done,* before the dukun pried it off and hurled it away, past the train tracks and the banana tree graves, into the cracks of the visible world and back from whence it came.

In the feverish aftermath, the shanty thick with the smell of burning organic matter, the dukun wrapped the board up in a bedsheet like a baby, like a body, and promised to find a way to destroy it. He also asked for more money than they had brought, far more than a younger, dumber Theo would have found remotely reasonable, but it didn't matter anymore—the lightness and freedom and distance he felt from that terrible bloody presence was so great that the dukun could have asked for the deed to their house and he would have given it freely.

"You should be careful the next few days," the dukun said, lighting another cigarette as a neighborhood rooster prematurely announced sunrise. "Just to make sure."

"I know," he said, but it was hard to keep the happiness from his voice when he couldn't remember ever being able to breathe so deeply, to inhale so much of the sweetness of the day.

***

Nelly Hartono sat in the Hotel des Tropiques with her sunglasses on, waiting to repay her family's debt, watching a lounge singer prepare the evening's songs—"Can't Help Falling in Love"?—and trying to hold steady to the collar of the wounded monster that sat where her heart used to be, stretching out her diaphragm, breaking her ribs.

A few Americans in cheap suits—Embassy staff—wandered by. The one woman, Deputy Chief of Mission Christine McGrath, stopped when she saw Nelly and awkwardly outstretched her hand, between a touch and a handshake. "Mrs. Hartono. I'm so sorry about your husband."

Theo had left their house the morning after his exorcism promising that he was going to make things right. She assumed he was talking about Operation White Dove, and she warned him—*don't do anything foolish*—but when was the last time Theo listened to her? He didn't come home that night, and still wasn't home the morning after, and she was biting her knuckles, debating whether or not to call the police, when one of his colleagues from the

Ministry arrived and said with a sad smile that there had been an accident. No blame, no fault. An accidental chain of events that Theo had instigated when he started voicing his most severe objections to the annexation of that poor, bleeding little Portuguese colony. So yes, what naturally followed was an accident. When you anger the bull, getting gored certainly isn't the bull's fault.

"Thank you," said Nelly. "I'm sure Theo is in a better place now."

She had fought to see him, in the hospital or the police station or wherever they had him, but they told her no, better if she didn't, Theo didn't look like himself, a knife had been used, his throat had been cut, both sides, he had practically been *decapitated*. "And you need to calm down," they said, "for your son." She got the message, though she didn't know what was left for her and Dino now that she was worse than a widow, and Dino worse than fatherless.

Christine McGrath nodded curtly and rejoined her posse. As soon as they were gone, the dukun slunk out of the shadows and sat down next to her, wearing a frown so deep it seemed to have been carved into the bone. She slipped him the money they owed him in an envelope, but he pushed it back to her. "Keep it," he said, "for your boy's schooling."

"It's a debt," Nelly said.

"I don't want it, Mrs. Hartono."

Shivering a little, she took the money back, nestled it in with what little she had left to her name. "What happened to the board? Did you figure out how to destroy it?"

"I threw it into the sea," the dukun sighed. "Hopefully it finds its way back to America."

Instead she imagined it being carried away on gentle waves to the little Portuguese colony, their newest little Portuguese province, finding a home amongst the battered separatists, again birthing something at once beautiful and powerful—another blonde nuclear missile, aimed straight at Nusantara. Of course she had known about Alice. Even if his secretary hadn't told her the gory details, she had known by the way his gaze searched the empty horizon, by the way he was never present even lying in bed beside her, that there had been someone else. At the piano, the lounge singer had chosen the night's poison: "You Are Always On My Mind."

"What interesting times we live in," Nelly said, with a small, indecipherable smile.

COPYRIGHT ACKNOWLEDGMENTS

"...a brilliant Cthonic horror fantasia full of creepy religion, grief, pain, sorrow and snakes." –Gemma Files, author of *Experimental Film*

When reporter Cora Mayburn is assigned to cover a story about a snake-handling cult in rural Appalachia, she is dismayed, for the world of cruel fundamentalist stricture, repression, glossolalia, and abuse is something she has long since put behind her in favor of a more tolerant urban existence.

As Cora begins to uncover the secrets concealed by a veneer of faith and tradition, something ancient and long concealed begins to awaken. What secrets do the townsfolk know? What might the handsome young pastor be hiding? What will happen when occulted horrors writhe to the surface, when pallid and forgotten things rise to reclaim the Earth?

Will Cora–and the earth–survive? The answers–and pure terror–can only be found in one place: *Beneath.*

Trade Paperback, 314 pp, $16.99

ISBN-13: 978-1-939905-29-1

http://www.wordhorde.com

"Bulkin serves up cerebral horror with plenty of bite."
—*Publishers Weekly* (starred review)

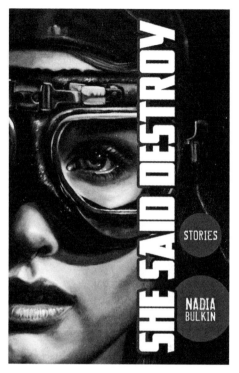

Word Horde presents the debut collection from critically-acclaimed Weird Fiction author Nadia Bulkin. Dreamlike, poignant, and unabashedly socio-political, *She Said Destroy* includes three stories nominated for the Shirley Jackson Award, four included in Year's Best anthologies, and one original tale.

"Weird fiction has been stuck in the era of new-fangled radio sets and fifteen-cent pulp magazines for ninety years. Finally, Nadia Bulkin has come to drag us kicking and screaming into the horrors of The Endless Now with a collection of hip, ultra-contemporary, politically astute, and chilling stories."
–Nick Mamatas, author of *I Am Providence*

Format: Trade Paperback, 258 pp, $16.99

ISBN-13: 978-1-939905-33-8

http://www.wordhorde.com

"…an excellent read for those who enjoy myths and legends of all kinds." —*Publishers Weekly* (starred review)

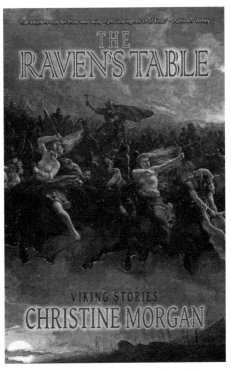

For a decade, author Christine Morgan's Viking stories have delighted readers and critics alike, standing apart from the anthologies they appeared in. Now, Word Horde brings you *The Raven's Table*, the first-ever collection of Christine Morgan's Vikings, from "The Barrow-Maid" to "Aerkheim's Horror" and beyond. These tales of adventure, fantasy, and horror will rouse your inner Viking.

"…stories that will make you want to don your helm, sword and shield before riding off into battle." —*The Grim Reader*

Format: Trade Paperback, 306 pp, $15.99

ISBN-13: 978-1-939905-27-7

http://www.wordhorde.com

"*This Is Spinal Tap* meets *The Thing* meets *From Beyond*."
— David James Keaton, author of *The Last Projector*

Codger Burton, bassist and lyricist for Frivolous Black,
the heaviest heavy metal band to ever come out of the
UK, awakens to find his hotel snowed in, his band mates
evacuated, and monsters roaming the halls. Looks like
Codger picked the wrong week to quit using cocaine.
From the twisted mind of Tony McMillen comes the
hilarious rock and roll horror of *An Augmented Fourth*,
a novel of the Lord of Low End.

Trade Paperback, 314 pp, $15.99
ISBN-13: 978-1-939905-31-4
http://www.wordhorde.com

WINNER OF THE BRAM STOKER AWARD FOR SUPERIOR ACHIEVEMENT IN A NOVEL.

The Fisherman is an epic, yet intimate, horror novel.
Langan channels M. R. James, Robert E. Howard, and Norman Maclean.
What you get is *A River Runs Through It*...Straight to hell.
—Laird Barron, author of *X's for Eyes*

THE
FISHERMAN
A NOVEL

JOHN
LANGAN

THIS IS HORROR NOVEL OF THE YEAR 2016

In upstate New York, in the woods around Woodstock, Dutchman's Creek flows out of the Ashokan Reservoir. Steep-banked, fast-moving, it offers the promise of fine fishing, and of something more, a possibility too fantastic to be true. When Abe and Dan, two widowers who have found solace in each other's company and a shared passion for fishing, hear rumors of the Creek, and what might be found there, the remedy to both their losses, they dismiss it as just another fish story. Soon, though, the men find themselves drawn into a tale as deep and old as the Reservoir. It's a tale of dark pacts, of long-buried secrets, and of a mysterious figure known as Der Fisher: the Fisherman. It will bring Abe and Dan face to face with all that they have lost, and with the price they must pay to regain it.

Trade Paperback, 282 pp, $16.99

ISBN-13: 978-1-939905-21-5

http://www.wordhorde.com

THIS IS HORROR SHORT STORY
COLLECTION OF THE YEAR 2016

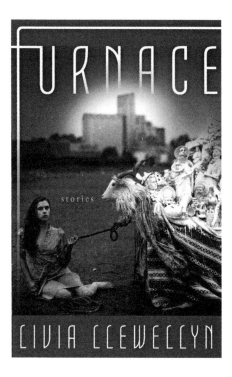

Horror fiction has long celebrated and explored the twin engines driving human existence. Call them what you like: Sex and Death, Love and Destruction, Temptation and Terror. While many may strive to reach the extremes, few authors manage to find the beauty that rests in the liminal space between these polar forces, the shuddering ecstasy encased within the shock. And then there's Livia Llewellyn, an author praised for her dark, stirring, evocative prose and disturbing, personal narratives.

Lush, layered, multifaceted, and elegant, the thirteen tales comprising *Furnace* showcase why Livia Llewellyn has been lauded by scholars and fans of weird fiction alike, and why she has been nominated multiple times for the Shirley Jackson Award and included in year's best anthologies. These are exquisite stories, of beauty and cruelty, of pleasure and pain, of hunger, and of sharp teeth sinking into tender flesh.

Format: Trade Paperback, 210 pp, $14.99

ISBN-13: 978-1-939905-17-8

http://www.wordhorde.com

Photo Credit: Raymond Lawrason

ABOUT THE EDITOR

ROSS E. LOCKHART is an author, anthologist, bookseller, editor, and publisher. A lifelong fan of supernatural, fantastic, speculative, and weird fiction, Lockhart is a veteran of small-press publishing, having edited scores of well-regarded novels of horror, fantasy, and science fiction.

Lockhart edited the anthologies *The Book of Cthulhu I* and *II*, *Tales of Jack the Ripper*, *The Children of Old Leech: A Tribute to the Carnivorous Cosmos of Laird Barron* (with Justin Steele), *Giallo Fantastique*, *Cthulhu Fhtagn!*, and *Eternal Frankenstein*. He is the author of *Chick Bassist*. Lockhart lives in Petaluma, California, with his wife Jennifer, hundreds of books, and Elinor Phantom, a Shih Tzu moonlighting as his editorial assistant.

Visit him online at www.haresrocklots.com